I0574152

THE SEVENTH KEY

A PARANORMAL WOMEN'S FICTION ROMANCE NOVEL

MICHELLE M. PILLOW

MICHELLEPILLOW.COM

The Seventh Key © Copyright 2022 by Michelle M. Pillow

First Printing November 29, 2022

Published by The Raven Books LLC

ISBN 978-1-62501-280-7

ALL RIGHTS RESERVED.

All books copyrighted to the author and may not be resold or given away without written permission from the author, Michelle M. Pillow.

This novel is a work of fiction. Any and all characters, events, and places are of the author's imagination and should not be confused with fact. Any resemblance to persons, living or dead, or events or places is merely coincidence.

Michelle M. Pillow® is a registered trademark of The Raven Books LLC

Unlucky number seven.

Nina Cole thought escaping a serial killer would be the hardest thing she ever had to face. When a reporter comes sniffing around wanting her to relive the trauma, she feels she has no choice but to pack up and move to a place where no one knows her. Starting over in her forties is easier said than done. Bad memories aren't the only thing chasing her. The killer might be in jail, but now it looks like something much more sinister from beyond the grave is hunting her.

Fortunately, there seems to be no shortage of magical assistance in Freewild Cove. But will it be enough? Can her new friends and a secret love interest help Nina survive the latest chapter in her unlucky life?

ORDER OF MAGIC SERIES

Second Chance Magic
Third Time's A Charm
The Fourth Power
The Fifth Sense
The Sixth Spell
The Seventh Key
The Eighth Potion

Visit MichellePillow.com for details!

AUTHOR UPDATES

Join the Reader Club Mailing List to stay informed
about new books, sales, contests and preorders!

http://michellepillow.com/author-updates/

To the Pillow Fighter Fan Club

AUTHOR NOTE

Being an author in my 40s, I am thrilled to be a part of this Paranormal Women's Fiction #PWF project. Older women kick ass. We know things. We've been there. We are worthy of our own literature category. We also have our own set of issues that we face—empty nests, widows, divorces, menopause, health concerns, etc—and these issues deserve to be addressed and embraced in fiction.

Growing older is a real part of life. Women friendships matter. Women matter. Our thoughts and feelings matter.

If you love this project as much as I do, be sure to spread the word to all your reader friends and let the vendors where you buy your books know you want to see a special category listing on their sites for 40+ heroines in Paranormal Women's Fiction and Romance.

Happy Reading!

Michelle M. Pillow

PRAISE FOR MICHELLE M. PILLOW

For Books in the *Order of Magic* Series

"[T]he cast of women and their bond resonates. This is a delight." *Publishers Weekly*

"The perfect combination of spine-tingling magic, paranormal fun, and the strength of female friendships. Michelle M. Pillow delivers an emotionally powerful, must-have read." - *K.F. Breene, Wall Street Journal, USA TODAY, and Washington Post Bestselling Author*

"Michelle M. Pillow's Second Chance Magic proves that sometimes all it takes to get a second chance after a massive betrayal, is a little luck, a lot of magic, and the help of your best friends." - *Mandy M. Roth, NY Times & USA TODAY Bestselling Author*

"Second Chance Magic starts with a bang and does not slow down! It's a beautifully written story of starting over and finding your inner power. Highly recommended." - *Elizabeth Hunter, USA*

TODAY *Bestselling Author of the Elemental Mysteries*

"Michelle M. Pillow brings us yet another hilariously touching story, this one set in the world of paranormal women's fiction, and you won't want to put it down. I know I didn't! Then again, she had me at séance." - *NY Times Bestselling Author Darynda Jones*

"When the past and the present merge...awesome author Michelle Pillow brings secrets from the grave and other things that go bump in the night into a fantastic story of second chances in the second act of life." - *Jana DeLeon, NY Times, USA TODAY, & Wall Street Journal Bestselling Author*

"Delightfully heartfelt and filled with emotion. Psychic powers, newly discovered magic, and a troublesome ex who comes back from the grave. Michelle M. Pillow delivers a wonderfully humorous start to a new paranormal women's fiction romance series." - *Robyn Peterman, NY Times and USA TODAY Bestselling Author*

"Second Chance Magic is full of heart and everything I love in a paranormal tale. Great friends, second chances, and physic powers... what's not to love?" - *Deanna Chase, NYT and USA Today Best-selling Author*

CHAPTER ONE

PROLOGUE

SALLYVILLE, North Carolina

The slap of wet pavement under her feet echoed over the empty sidewalk. Every other step caused a sting to shoot up her leg. The thin material of the pale blue hospital gown did little to hide her from the elements as she passed between awnings into the rain. It clung to her skin, stained pink in areas from the injuries beneath.

Her mind drifted through a terrible haze, and she couldn't remember her name, where she was, or why. All she knew was she had to run, had to get away from the thing hurting her.

It became impossible to tell where her pain radiated from. Breathing too deeply hurt. The wet material clinging to her back grated like metal against raw skin. Her arm felt too heavy to lift.

Each awning gave reprieve from the weather, except for the wet puddles gathering on the uneven surfaces. Light came from one of the windows. She passed through it, unable to focus on anything happening inside of the building. All she could do was move forward—rain, awning, rain, awning, soaked, wet, soaked...

Street.

She stopped at the curb, confused at the break in her pattern. Rain pelted her from above. The sound of a car caught her attention and she stared at two looming headlights. They grew from the darkness, prompting a fearful reaction as she darted in front of it to run past.

Tires squealed as the car slammed on its brakes. Then, darkness.

CHAPTER TWO

Freewild Cove, North Carolina, Sixteen Months Later...

Lucky.

Nina Cole didn't feel lucky, but people loved to use that word to describe her. Lucky to have survived. Lucky to have gotten away. Lucky that Robert Chester Teeter was in jail awaiting trial. Lucky number seven.

Fucking lucky.

Nightmares didn't feel very lucky when she had to relive them every night. Or when she jumped at every accidental brush of someone's hand. Too traumatized to date or walk alone at night or sit with her back to a door where she couldn't see everything. She felt watched even when alone. Like now.

A short string of dust floating in the light captured her attention and held it. The sunlight crept between the slats of a blind from the window of her new rental house. The dust disappeared into a shadow.

She'd been there three days and, though she was surrounded by her meager furniture, it felt like a vacation home. Cardboard boxes lined one of the bedroom walls, waiting to be unpacked. A few of them were open, draped with shirts from when she'd dug through them. A black garbage bag filled with her jeans and socks was torn open on the floor.

Nina found it difficult to summon the energy to unpack. She found it difficult to do a lot of things lately. What if this town didn't work out? What if everyone realized who she was? What if reporters came sniffing around her front lawn again?

The district attorney had said she would try to keep Nina out of the papers. Delany meant well, but it would take an act of pure magic to keep what happened out of the news. And Nina had stopped believing in magic around the same time she learned the truth about Santa Claus.

Freewild Cove felt about as safe as she could get. It wasn't home, and she had no reason to move there, which meant people wouldn't think to look for her.

Safe.

Lucky.

People put more meaning into those words than they should. Safe and lucky were more an illusion than an actual state of being.

"Safe," she whispered. "Sure. Safe."

Experience told her no one was safe. Ever. It didn't matter what kind of life you had lived, or whether or not you went to church. There were no guarantees. There was no safety in numbers. Dressing conservatively and carrying pepper spray did not promise safe passage through life.

Reaching for her phone, Nina clicked the screen on and then dragged her thumb down the surface to refresh her internet search. The same news articles that had been there for the last week reappeared.

"Captured Serial Killer. Robert Chester Teeter arrested and held without bail..."

Nina breathed a sigh of relief. No news was good news. She pushed up on the bed and frowned at the boxes. If she left them packed, she could move out faster. If she unpacked them, she could pretend life was getting back to normal.

Her therapist had suggested Nina focus on the things she could control—on a task in front of her that could be done that brought her life forward.

As she had every day since moving in, she negotiated with herself. "One box a day."

Nina went to a box labeled dresses and tore open the top. She looped her hand under the stack of clothing and pulled them out. They were still on hangers, so all she had to do was place them in the closet.

"There. One box done." She grabbed the empty box and carried it down the hallway to the living room, where she dropped it next to a stack of empties.

Light tried to invade through the drawn curtains. She used to love the morning sun but felt safer with the drapes closed. Even now, she felt like someone was looking at her, peeping at her through some hole she had yet to notice.

But what if it wasn't a hole? A chill worked over her, and she rubbed her arms. Her new landlord, Heather Harrison, didn't seem like the type to put hidden cameras everywhere but there were several thriller movies made with that very concept.

"Heather is a nice lady," Nina said to herself. "I'm projecting my fears. That's normal. I give myself permission to relax."

The self-talk wasn't working. Maybe she needed a new therapist.

Nina stared at the empty boxes, forgetting for a moment what she should be doing. Was this what her life had become? Paralyzed in each moment? Trapped by her own thoughts? Imagining the worst possible scenario?

"I give myself permission to shake off the nightmares."

It didn't work. The feelings lingered.

"I give myself permission to find coffee."

Nina turned toward the coffee pot. The kitchen was separated from the living room by a passthrough window. The pot sat on the counter where she'd left it. She stared at it for a long moment before finally making the effort to go turn it on.

As she walked into the kitchen, she mumbled, "I give myself permission to eat junk food. Oh, wait, I don't have any—"

A loud knock sounded on the door, causing her to jump in surprise. Her heartbeat kicked up a notch and she had to take a deep breath to try to calm down. She froze in the doorway to the kitchen and stared across the living room at the door.

The knock sounded again. She saw a shadow fall against the back of the curtains, subtle but there.

Nina didn't know anyone in town. She had told no one where to find her. Utilities were all hooked up so it shouldn't be a maintenance worker of any kind. The landlord had no reason to stop by.

"Go away," she mouthed.

The knock sounded a third time.

Creeping barefoot over the carpet, she went toward the door. She glanced around her home to ensure she was alone, still unable to shake the feeling of being watched. Her heart did not slow.

Nina leaned her ear against the door.

"Maybe she's not awake?" a woman suggested.

"It's ten in the morning," another answered.

"Maybe I should leave this on the porch," a third added.

"Just give her a minute," Heather said before another knock sounded.

Her landlord?

Nina glanced down at her old t-shirt and yoga pants. She finger-brushed her hair back from her face before unlocking the door.

"Hello," she said as she peeked outside. She blocked the door with her foot to keep it from opening too wide.

"Hi, Nina. I hope it's a good time for us to come by." Heather had a straightforward manner that Nina appreciated. Her flannel shirt was rolled at the sleeves as if she was ready to get to work, with a small notebook and pen in the front pocket. She had pulled her hair back into a ponytail. When she smiled, it looked like she meant it. There was no calculation in her gaze, no sense of hidden meanings in her words. She didn't glance around or study her phone like there was some place else she'd rather be.

Seeing that the group of women were looking expectantly at her, Nina said, "I'm still unpacking. The house is a mess."

"We wanted to welcome you to Freewild Cove." One of the women held up a basket. Her reddish-blonde hair was piled on top of her head in a curly bun. "I'm Lorna Addams. We made you muffins."

"Oh, um..." Nina hesitated before letting the door open all the way. She reached for the offered basket, but the next woman's words stopped her.

"By we, she means her." The lady who stepped forward to push her way inside looked ready for a boardroom. Long wavy brown hair flowed around her shoulders as if she'd just stepped out of a salon, and her business suit appeared new like she'd just taken it off a very expensive clothing rack. "I'm Vivien Stone. I didn't bake. Trust me, that's a good thing. Lorna is amazing."

Nina felt compelled to step aside to invite them in. It was more a reaction to Vivien's assertive presence than the desire for company. Vivien, Lorna, and Heather stepped inside. Almost embarrassed, Nina looked at the stack of empty boxes. She said the only thing she could think of. "I'm still moving in."

"Hi. I'm Sue Jewel. Latte?" A redhead lifted a to-go cup toward Nina as she paused in the doorway.

"Oh, um, thank you," Nina answered, taking the cup. She gestured to herself. "Nina Cole."

"I'll put these in the kitchen." Lorna carried the basket into the kitchen.

"If you're done with these boxes, I can drop them off at the recycling center. I'll be driving by the bins on my way to work," Heather offered.

"Oh, yeah, thanks." Nina glanced around in confusion as the women moved about the room. Though she'd agreed, she didn't want to give up the boxes. What if she had to leave?

"We know how tiring moving can be," Sue said.

Vivien looked at the ceiling. "Heather, you did an amazing job in here. The room feels so much bigger after being opened up to the kitchen."

"I thought so." Heather broke down a box so that it would lie flat. "Martin had to rewire..."

"I hope you like chocolate muffins," Lorna called from the kitchen, "but if not, there are blueberry, apple cinnamon, pumpkin..."

"She's renowned for her chocolate," Vivien said. "Try the chocolate."

"Where would you like us to get started?" Sue asked.

They all talked over each other. There was too much activity.

"I'm sorry?" Nina tried to follow what was happening.

"I can heat one up for you if you like," Lorna offered.

"What color is this?" Vivien asked.

"Natural bark," Heather answered.

"It looks like milk chocolate." Vivien ran her hand over the wall. "Delicious."

"Don't lick the walls," Heather muttered.

"We thought we'd help you unpack," Sue said. "Heather mentioned you were on your own. She saw you unloading the moving truck you rented. It can be overwhelming. I'm very good at organizing."

"*Mm-hm,*" Lorna agreed from the kitchen doorway. "Sue has a talent for it."

"I..." As the heat seeped into her fingers, Nina shifted the coffee in her hands. Although it smelled amazing, she would not drink anything a stranger handed her in an open container. "Thank you, but no."

"Are you sure?" Sue asked. "We don't mind."

"I can see not wanting strangers digging through your belongings," Heather said. "No worries. It was just an offer."

"We ladies have to stick together," Lorna added.

"No, that's not it, is it?" Vivien tilted her head as she studied Nina. Her eyes moved as if reading her expression.

Nina tried not to show any emotion at the inspection. Her reaction to them had nothing to do with not wanting to make friends and everything to do with the whirlwind of activity they brought with them. Their energy filled the place, making it hard for Nina to breathe.

"Your worries go deeper, don't they?" Vivien gave a sad smile and lifted a hand toward her. "What happened? Something bad, right? No. Worse than bad."

Nina frowned. So that was it. They somehow knew about her past, and they came for the gossip. It wasn't like the woman could psychically deduce something was wrong.

But how? Her name wasn't in the papers.

Or was it? She should have checked for her name, not Teeter's.

"Heather, I'm sorry. I don't think this house is

going to work out for me." Nina tried not to consider the six-month rental agreement or the security deposit she'd be forfeiting.

"What? Why? Is there an issue?" Heather instantly began inspecting the room. "I have other properties. I'm happy to help you move into one of those instead as soon as they're ready. All the completed units are occupied, but if you can give me a few weeks..."

"I mean, this town. I don't think this town is going to work for me," Nina corrected.

"Oh, no, did a job fall through?" Lorna asked. "I'm sure we can help with that."

"It's not fancy, but Jameson was talking about hiring extra help at the coffee shop," Sue offered.

"No. It's not a job," Vivien answered for her.

Nina took a step back away from the woman. Vivien seemed so sure in her assessments. Nina didn't like the invasion or the presumption.

"It's me. I'm making her uncomfortable." Vivien folded her hands in front of her. "Please forgive my familiarity. I sometimes get..."

"Nosy," Heather finished.

"Focused," Lorna said at the same time.

"Yes," Vivien agreed. "Both of those."

"You don't have to tell us your life story," Heather said. "Your business is your business."

Nina nodded. Maybe she had overreacted. Every nerve in her body was on constant edge. Her hand shook, and she set the coffee cup down on the countertop.

"There's nothing to tell," she lied.

"I doubt that," Lorna answered. "Well, if you won't let us help unpack, can I at least make you lunch?"

"I haven't been to the store," Nina said by way of denial.

"Great, we'll go out," Vivien suggested. "Show you the town."

Nina pulled nervously on the waist of her t-shirt. "My clothes are still packed."

Sue pulled her phone from her back pocket. "Pizza delivery should be open."

"I..." Nina glanced around at the expectant faces.

I don't have money.

I don't eat pizza. Ignore the pizza box in the trash.

"I'm running out of excuses," Nina finally finished.

"Good!" Vivien exclaimed. "Lorna, will you do the honors?"

"Nina, what kind do you like?" Lorna asked.

"Anything," Nina answered, not wanting to make the decision. But when Lorna kept looking at her, she said, "Barbeque chicken or Mediterranean or anything with a white sauce."

"Interesting." Lorna gave a nod of approval.

"Cheese sticks," Heather said.

"Dessert sticks," Vivien added.

"Got it and got it," Lorna answered.

"Garlic bread," Sue said. "Oh, and those little puffy things."

"Are more people coming?" Nina asked.

The ladies shook their heads.

"Leftovers mean we don't have to cook later," Sue said.

"Pepperoni calzone," Heather said. "Extra marinara."

"Oh, two of those!" Vivien inserted.

"I'm calling now," Lorna stated, holding her hand over her free ear as she listened to her phone. "Orders are closed."

"Oh, sodas," Heather added.

Lorna waved her hand at Heather.

"I see a box marked kitchen." Sue pointed toward the corner where boxes were stacked in a pile. "Plates?"

"In one of those," Nina answered.

"May I unpack?" Sue started for the boxes and stopped mid-gesture.

"Sure." Nina knew she was outmaneuvered. It wasn't just their enthusiastic nature and fast way of talking. There was that energy humming in the air as if it bounced off them and electrified the room.

Nina's palm itched, and she rubbed it as she watched them. Vivien opened the blinds. The tiny specs of dust stirred in the sunlight, almost seeming to sparkle. Sue pulled open the box, breaking the seal of packing tape.

"Guys." Sue stared into the box. She slowly reached in to pull out one of Nina's bowls. The porcelain looked daintier than it was, with tiny flowers painted along the rim.

"Yeah?" Heather crossed to look at the bowl.

Vivien joined them. "So, we were right."

Nina frowned. Right about what?

"I don't think it's worth anything. It is from a dish set my mother had since I was a little girl." Nina tried to look inside the dish without moving from where she stood.

Sue carried it to her. Something clinked softly inside it. "I found your ring."

"You should put it on so you don't lose it," Vivien added.

Nina glanced to see a ring with a large oval stone on it. She shook her head. "That's not mine. I don't wear jewelry. Earrings sometimes, but that's it."

The energy in the air became more robust, as if lightning would appear over her head at any moment. A sense of panic filled her as Sue leaned closer. Nina took a step back to keep her distance.

"They said thirty minutes." Lorna rejoined the group. "But Jimmy is driving, so that means it'll be at least forty. Unless he stops to see his girlfriend, then an hour."

"They broke up," Vivien said.

"Again?" Heather shook her head and sighed.

"His dumbass told her he wanted a hall pass when he was married," Vivien said. "She threw him out of her car."

"I'll set the ring right here, so you don't lose it." Sue put the bowl on the passthrough counter. She returned to the box and began pulling out stacks of dishes.

"Excuse me." Nina backed into the hallway and ducked into her bathroom.

Locking herself in, she took several deep breaths and stared into the mirror. The word banshee came to mind. Streaks of white hair had spread through the brunette, especially at the temples. Someone had told her trauma would do that, but it could have just been age too. Or the fact she'd stopped going to the hairdresser.

Even her hazel eyes looked dull, like a sheen of *blah* had just taken up residence on her face.

When had she started looking so old? And tired? She was only forty-six.

It was like she'd blinked, and suddenly she had smile lines and wrinkles.

How could she have developed smile lines when she hadn't been smiling?

"You can't hide in here," she told her reflection.

Nina grabbed a black scrunchie to tame her hair and quickly washed her face. It helped a little, but she again found herself staring at her reflection.

"You can't stay in here. They're nice ladies. They're not here to harm you. This is what small-town people do."

She waited for her reflection to answer and then figured it was lucky when it didn't.

Nina cracked open the door and listened.

"...too many boxes?" Sue asked. "I don't want to overstep."

"Maybe we were too pushy." Lorna sounded worried. "We can be a little overwhelming, especially when we're excited. Do you think the muffins were too much? I want her to feel welcome."

"There is a ring," Vivien stated as if that was an actual answer to anything.

"I have to trust my gut on this one," Heather said. "She—"

"Shh," Vivien shushed. "Where is that Jimmy? I'm starving."

"Have a muffin," Lorna said.

"You should make cheesy calzone muffins," Vivien answered.

"Interesting thought," Lorna drawled.

Nina came out of the bathroom wondering what Heather had started to say before Vivien redirected the conversation.

"Kitchen's unpacked." Sue motioned to where the pile of boxes had been minutes before.

Nina glanced at the empty space. The boxes were broken down and stacked in a pile near the door. With her one-box-a-day plan, this put her about a week ahead of schedule. "All of them?"

"Yeah, we're not kidding when we say she's magic when it comes to organizing." Vivien's smile seemed a little strange as if she laughed at a private joke.

The house appeared cleaner, but she was unsure

if that was because the kitchen boxes were cleared away. The dust specs were no longer floating in the light. The little swirls she had drawn in the dust on the kitchen bar were wiped away. Instead, place settings had been set up. Her mother's bowl holding the ring had been positioned within view next to one of the plates.

Nina stared at the ring and resisted the urge to pick it up. She wasn't sure how it had gotten into her moving box.

"It's pretty," Lorna said.

Nina frowned. "Excuse me?"

"The ring. It's pretty," she clarified.

"Looks like an antique," Heather added, touching a ring on her own hand. The jewelry seemed out of place for someone in flannel and work boots looking like she was about to take on a construction project.

Nina wasn't sure why her gaze moved from hand to hand. Each of them wore what looked to be antique rings. Her suspicious mind conjured up all kinds of conspiracies. Why were the women here? What was it with the rings? Why did they seem to want her to put one on so badly? She knew it didn't belong to her, and no amount of gaslighting would make her believe it did. What was their angle?

Her eyes moved to the coffee cup they had brought. She wanted it but couldn't bring herself to drink it. She hadn't seen the liquid poured, and there was no way to force them to taste test it first without looking like a crazy lady.

But maybe she *was* a crazy lady.

"If you all like it so much, take it," Nina said. "It's not my ring. Maybe the last tenant left it here."

"It's not..." Lorna looked at Heather as if desperate for support.

Heather gave a helpless shrug.

Lorna gestured toward Nina and jerked her head as if silently telling Heather to speak.

Heather sighed. "Nina, do you believe in powers beyond our control?"

Nina felt the tension in her chest ease and gave a small laugh. "Oh, you all want to convert me. That's what this is. Listen, thank you for the offer but I'm not interested in changing religions. I was born Baptist, and though I'm not exactly practicing, I'm not looking to join another club."

She crossed to the front door and held it open. "But thank you for stopping—"

"We're not..." This time Lorna looked at Vivien for help. "Should we just...?"

"We're not converting you. We're here to help

you. It doesn't make sense now, but it will. You're going to have to trust us." Vivien's tone was blunter than Heather's. "Did anything strange happen to you before you moved here?"

Nina stared at the woman, not answering. The tightness returned. She didn't want to talk about any of this.

"Just keep an open mind and listen to what we're about to say," Sue said. "Have you experienced anything strange?"

Like four women barging into her home and trying to get her to put on a stupid ring?

"Electrical surges? Televisions that come on by themselves?" Lorna asked.

"The electric seems fine here," Nina answered.

"Sounds you can't explain? Objects appearing to have moved on their own? Strange smells?" Sue swept her hand over the countertop and toyed with the place settings.

Nina remembered the feeling of being drugged, of her vision swimming and hallucinations that didn't make any sense.

"Ghosts," Vivien inserted candidly. "Disembodied voices. Demonic—"

"I think you should leave." Nina continued to

hold the door. "I don't think this whole haze the new girl in town is funny."

"No, we're not hazing—" Sue tried to say.

"Please, I'm sorry. I can't do this now." Nina gestured at the door. "Thank you for the coffee and muffins and the welcome, but I have a busy schedule and..."

"We understand," Heather stated for the group. "We'll go."

Sue and Lorna left first.

Vivien paused in the doorway. "Pizza is paid for. Keep it. Enjoy. Welcome to Freewild Cove."

Heather picked up the stack of cardboard and carried it out. "You have my number. Call if you need anything. *Anything*."

"Thank you." Nina couldn't help but feel a little rude as she shut the door and locked it, but she didn't invite them back in. She was the first to admit her social skills were off, and it was difficult to read people's intentions, but those ladies were odd.

Standing with her back against the door, she waited for the sound of their cars driving into the distance before moving to close the blinds. As the room darkened and silence resumed, she felt a little better.

"Coffee," she whispered, heading toward the

kitchen to make a pot. She grabbed the to-go cup and dumped the latte in the sink. It smelled amazing, but she needed to remain vigilant. She didn't know these women, and even children knew you didn't take candy from strangers. That was one lesson she'd learned the hard way.

CHAPTER THREE

G HOSTS.

The idea was utter nonsense, but Nina still found herself staring at the ceiling, listening for the thud she had heard moments before. She held a slice of cold pizza in her hand. Since it came from a restaurant and was meant for all the ladies, she decided she could risk eating it.

That, and it was the only food in the house.

Her mother's bowl was turned upside down on the counter to hide the ring. For the life of her, she couldn't figure out why they wanted her to put it on. Was it some joke or challenge? Or a scavenger hunt? Whoever convinced her won their game?

"You have trust issues," she muttered, "and ghosts aren't real."

As if to dispute the claim, another thud sounded overhead.

Nina set the pizza down on a plate. She used to love meeting people. Growing up in her neighborhood, they always had potlucks and street parties. As an adult, she had easily talked to new people.

That all stopped the night she got *lucky*.

Fear rode around inside her chest like a hard knot that stopped her from catching her breath. It paralyzed her and made her want to sit in dark corners where no one could find her. She didn't want to be alone, but she couldn't be around people.

There were times when she didn't feel as if she were in her body. Nothing mattered, and everything around her was purgatory. Maybe she hadn't survived.

Sliding her plate aside, she lifted the bowl to uncover the ring. The jewelry was more prominent than she'd normally wear on the rare occasion she felt the need. She touched it with the tip of her finger and felt a tiny static shock.

Another thud sounded. She tried not to look up. Reason would tell her that each house made its own noises, and it took a while to learn those sounds.

Her phone rang. The sudden noise caused her to jolt in surprise.

She looked toward the bedroom. Only a few people had her new number.

It continued to ring.

"You have to answer," she told herself. "It could be important."

Nina forced her feet to move. Daily life had become a chore.

She grabbed her cell phone off the nightstand and glanced at the screen before answering, "Yes?"

"Nina, it's Jacob Paddock."

The introduction wasn't necessary. She recognized his voice. He was an investigator for the district attorney's office and one of the few people who knew her story. In fact, he'd been one of the first to get her to talk about it. He'd visited with her in the hospital right after she'd been found.

"Where are you?" Jacob asked.

"I don't want to say." Nina pulled the charger out of the phone and headed back toward the living room.

"You sound worried. Are you safe?"

"I think so." She glanced at the ceiling.

"Are you at home? I'm on my way over," Jacob sounded adamant.

"I'm not there. A reporter was sniffing around.

They followed someone from the DA's office to my house."

"Are you sure?" Jacob knew how paranoid she could be, especially right after it happened. She'd seen people following her everywhere.

"Yes. They came to my door asking all kinds of questions. I lied and said I had gone for a deposition subpoena for a minor workplace accident. I didn't want to risk being outed, so I," she sighed and mumbled, "left. I moved."

"Hotel?"

"No." She bounced the tip of her finger against the ring to see if it would shock her again. It didn't.

"I need to talk to you."

"You *are* talking to me."

"Nina, please. I need to see you. My boss would feel better if I could assure him that I laid eyes on you."

"I rented a place out of town." She picked up the ring and examined the oval stone. "I'll come back when I must, but for now, it's better if people don't know where to find me. If they need me, tell them to have you call me."

"Actually, full disclosure, I don't care what the boss wants. *I* would feel better if I could see you." Jacob was one of the few people she trusted. He'd

proven himself to her time and time again. "I promise, no one who doesn't need to know it will find out
your location from me, but I would like to talk to you
in person. Someone should know where you are. To
be sure you're safe."

Nina took a deep breath and nodded against the
phone. "All right. Just you. I rented a place in
Freewild Cove, but you don't have to—"

"I'll call you when I'm in town." Jacob hung up
before she could protest.

Nina set the phone down but kept the ring,
pinching it between her thumb and middle finger.
Her hand tingled, and the band flipped down over
the tip of her finger. Almost instantly, it slid down
her finger as if pushed by an invisible hand.

A chill worked over her, and the room darkened
as if clouds moved over the sun to block what little
light managed to make its way inside.

"Dammit." She tried to pull the ring off, but it
wouldn't slide past her knuckle. She turned it several
times, but the stubborn piece of jewelry refused to
move.

A louder thud sounded. This time it was
followed by the sound of heavy footsteps running
overhead. They made their way over to the square
attic access panel in the hallway ceiling.

Nina grabbed the phone.

The panel creaked as someone pried it open.

Screaming, she darted for the front door.

A figure dropped from the ceiling and landed on the floor with a gruff yell.

Panicked, she fumbled with the lock before managing to throw the door open. She ran, darting past her car as she took off barefoot down the street. The feel of the pavement was all too familiar and only caused her anxiety to worsen.

Nina didn't stop, didn't turn around to see who might be after her. All she could do was scream and run.

CHAPTER FOUR

NINA SAT in the back of the police cruiser, pressing her head against the window while straining to see what was happening. She pulled at the handle, but the door did not open. That didn't stop her from noisily flicking it. A metal grate kept her from attempting to crawl into the front.

"I did nothing wrong," she whispered, hating that they'd locked her in the back.

The red and blue flashing lights acted like a beacon to her new neighbors, bringing them out on their lawns to watch the show. A few of them pointed toward her like she was a criminal.

Nina flicked the latch harder. She leaned to look through the metal grates at the rental house. Officer

Carnac talked to Heather and a couple of other officers on the front steps.

Nina's feet ached from her barefoot run. The constant fear living inside her chest became a large, pulsing mass. It made waves of nausea rush over her stomach. Her throat tightened. She forced large, deep breaths, trying to keep the panic from rising. The first time she'd experienced a panic attack, she'd thought her heart was about to stop.

Warmth spread up her hand from the ring and brought with it a sense of calm. She took another deep breath, willing the anxiety to lessen. To her surprise, it did.

Nina watched as Heather and Officer Carnac walked toward her. She again tried the handle, not expecting it to open. The door popped open. Carnac looked surprised as she stepped out. He went to the door and flicked the handle a few times, testing why it let her out of the backseat of his cruiser.

"I'm not crazy." Nina knew that was probably the impression she'd given the officer when he'd picked her up in the middle of the road. She clutched her cell phone, turning it between her hands. "Someone was in the attic."

Heather looked like she wanted to speak, but Carnac cut her off.

"We believe you." He gave up on the door and pushed it closed. "We found evidence that someone has been living in the attic. They must have moved in while it was under construction. It happens more than you might think, especially during the pandemic. Homelessness has really hit people hard. They get desperate. I'm guessing your houseguest accidentally made a noise, got worried, and panicked as they tried to escape."

Why did the officer sound so calm? Nothing about what he said sounded normal.

"What kind of evidence?" Nina stared at the house. It didn't have a livable second floor—not that she had gone up to check the attic through the access panel.

"Empty soup cans, a nest of blankets," Carnac explained. "Common camp-out items. A bucket for... well, a bucket."

Again. So not normal.

Why was he looking at her like this happened all the time, and she should accept it?

"They call it phrogging," Carnac continued. "That's phrog with a P H, not an F. Though, I'm guessing technically they started as a squatter and then became a phrogger after you moved in."

"Phrogging?" Nina looked at Heather in confusion, wondering if this made any sense to her.

"When vagrants move into an occupied home and live there while the rightful inhabitants don't realize they have a guest," the officer clarified, his tone indicating he felt like an authority. She half expected him to pat her head and call her a little lady. "It's like a squatter but in a person's home. Or a houseguest who doesn't tell you he's staying over."

This couldn't be a real thing. It sounded like a sinister movie plot.

"Someone was living in the house with me?" Nina hugged her arms across her stomach. How could she not have known that? Or sensed something was wrong? "I've been in there for three days."

"He looks like he might have been in there for weeks," Carnac said.

"So, you caught him?" Nina looked at the neighbors still watching from their lawns. They had started to cluster into groups, and the murmur of their voices spread the gossip.

"No, but we're looking into it," he said. "He shouldn't be causing you any other problems. After they're found out, they don't normally come back."

Nina stared at the house. "I should never have moved here."

It would seem her lousy luck had followed her.

Her hand began to vibrate and ring. She automatically lifted her phone to look. Jacob was calling. She denied the call.

"Nina, I don't know what to say," Heather said. "There was never any indication that someone was staying there. I already have the guys coming over to check every inch of the place. We're putting new locks on all the doors. I'll even have a security system installed. Whatever you need."

Nina wanted to nod and say something reassuring. She wanted to agree that Heather's steps sounded reasonable for a landlord. She wanted to tell the officer that she trusted his assessment and thank him for making her feel safe.

But none of that was true.

"I can't live there." Nina wasn't made of money. She was already scrimping to make this move work. If Heather tried to force her to pay out the lease, she'd be...

Nina sighed. She'd be phrogging in someone's attic.

The thought would have been funny if it wasn't so dire.

Her phone began ringing again. She held up her

hand toward Heather. "Excuse me. I have to answer this."

Nina stepped away from the car to answer. "Jacob?"

Officer Carnac cleared his throat.

"I'm in town. Where are you?" he asked.

"I can't talk now. I have a phrog problem," she said.

"I think we have a bad connection. Did you say you have frogs? Reptile frogs as in ribbit?" Jacob sounded puzzled.

"Not exactly." Nina met the cop's eyes. He didn't appear too patient. "I really have to go."

"Where can we meet? I'm not leaving before I talk to you," he insisted.

"Um, coffee shop downtown." Nina turned to the side, ducking her head to avoid Carnac's stare.

"Which one?"

"I think there is only one," she said. "I might be a while."

"Ms. Cole," Carnac stated.

"I'll stay until close if I have to, but—"

"Ms. Cole," Carnac repeated louder.

Nina hung up on him, cutting off Jacob's words. "Yes?"

"You did the right thing leaving the premises.

Give us a call if anything else comes up or if you notice any missing items," Carnac said before turning to include Heather in his conversation. "The house is clear. You can go back inside. We'll be in touch."

"Thank you," Heather said.

They watched as the officer got into his cruiser. When Carnac was driving away, a neighbor tried to wave Heather over. "Do you know who it is?"

"No." Heather shook her head in denial. She motioned for Nina to follow her.

"I'm not comfortable staying—" Nina began.

"Let's talk inside before they converge." Heather took Nina's arm and walked toward the house. "Trust me. We'll never get away."

Nina didn't make eye contact with the neighbors as they hurried over the street to the house. She stepped up on the curb, balancing along the smoother path.

Heather went inside first and held open the door. As it closed, she said, "I don't know what to say. This has never happened in any of my properties before. I've never even heard of it happening in this town, and I've lived here my whole life."

Nina went to look down the hall, where the attic hatch was lying on the floor.

"I hear you when you say you can't be here. Of

course, don't worry about the lease." Heather peered around the home. "I can show you the other houses. They're not ready, but if you see one you like, I'll have everyone converge on it, and we'll get it done. Until then, you can stay in our guest room. We'd love to have you. We have plenty of space."

Nina thought about insisting on a hotel, but there were two problems with that idea. She couldn't afford it, and she didn't want to be alone.

Nina nodded. "Yes. Thank you."

"We'll take care of all the boxes," Heather said. "Just grab whatever you need, and we'll get out of here."

Nina looked at the phone in her hand. "I'll pack a bag."

She went to the bedroom, glancing through the ceiling hole to see the unfinished attic's wood beams. Her anxiety wasn't just from the houseguest. The phrog only amplified her fear.

What was this world coming to? Nowhere felt safe.

CHAPTER FIVE

OLD ANDERSON HOUSE.

That's what Heather had called her home. She'd mentioned it was built in 1883 and had gotten its name from the original owners. The Queen Anne style had been prevalent at the time. She even talked about her favorite part of the structure and the reason why she had wanted the house in the first place, a small cupola that served as a lookout toward the ocean.

All fascinating information if someone wanted, say, a historical tour of Freewild Cove or had an interest in bed-and-breakfasts. Nina did not care about the original windows or wooden balusters or the number of bedrooms. As long as a phrog wasn't up top living in the said cupola, that was a win.

Heather hurried up the porch and opened the door. "Come on in. We'll get you settled."

Nina was slow to follow.

"You remember my roommates," Heather said, motioning toward Lorna and Vivien.

"Great to see you again, Nina." Lorna sat on the living room couch where she folded a stack of towels. "Heather mentioned you'd be staying with us. Welcome!"

Vivien leaned against an archway, partially blocking the dining room. She picked at a muffin. "I'm sorry that it's under these circumstances. How weird is that to think someone was living in the attic?"

Nina nodded.

Vivien's expression fell. "I'm sorry. I didn't realize you were still so shaken up by it. Were you injured?"

"No. It's just..." Nina shrugged.

Vivien came into the room and handed her muffin to Lorna as she stared at Nina intently.

"This is..." Vivien lifted her hand and moved it in a circle to encompass Nina. "What is this cloud I'm seeing around you?"

Heather seemed sane. Nina wasn't sure she could say the same for the woman's friends. Asking about televisions turning on and off on their own? Disembodied voices? Ghosts? Demons? And now cloudy auras?

Life had enough scary in it without them adding the paranormal.

Vivien's hands started to shake. Her eyes widened and she breathed deeply. "You put the ring on."

Nina flexed her hand.

"I'm seeing it so much clearer. There's..." Vivien swiped at her eye as a tear surfaced and then touched her chest. "It's here, isn't it?"

"Viv, what's here?" Heather looked around the room before focusing on Nina. "I don't see anything."

Lorna held very still, her hand acting like a tray for the discarded muffin.

Vivien seemed to struggle with her words.

"Viv?" Heather insisted.

"Terror," Vivien finally whispered. "What the hell happened to you, Nina?"

"I don't know what you mean," Nina lied. Theatrics aside, it was clear Vivien was trying to get the story out of her.

"How can you even breathe?" Vivien balled a fist against her chest.

Nina's hand tingled and she stretched her

fingers. She twisted the ring back and forth, trying to get the blood flowing to her fingertip. "I don't know what you're talking about."

"Let's get you settled. The guest room is on the second floor," Heather said, motioning that Nina should follow her up.

"I can't do this." Nina shook her head and moved toward the door. She'd probably end up sleeping in her car, but they didn't need to know that. "I'm going to stay at a hotel. I'll make arrangements to get my boxes later."

"No," Vivien stated, the word coming out like a command. "Heather, don't let her leave."

"I think we have to have the conversation." Lorna set the muffin down on the coffee table and patted the couch next to her. "Nina, please have a seat."

Nina reached behind her back, searching for the doorknob.

"If you don't like what we have to say, I promise we'll leave you alone," Lorna added. "Please. What do you have to lose? We're not as insane as we may come across. Honest."

"I'll stand," Nina said, dropping her hand but not leaving the vicinity of the door.

"Vivien..." Lorna began. "Well, no, Heather is..."

"You think we'd be better at this by now." Heather shook her head and chuckled to herself.

"She's going to think we're crazy no matter what we say," Vivien stated. "So here goes. I'm psychic. Clairsentient to be exact. And claircognizant, if you must know the names, not that anyone ever recognizes them for what they are."

Nina stared at her. Okay, so maybe this wasn't so bad. Fake psychics were all over late-night television and the Renaissance Faire circuits. Wacky, but whatever.

"It means I'm empathic," Vivien explained. "I feel what other people feel, and I just understand things without them having to be said. It's a family trait. My ancestors were fortune-tellers for carnivals. They did tarot card readings, things like that. But don't ask me to predict your future or anything."

"Empathic," Nina repeated. Vivien was sensitive to others. Read micro-expressions. That wasn't too strange. "So, no talking to ghosts or anything?"

"Not without a spell." Vivien gave a small laugh.

Nina started to smile at the joke.

Vivien pointed at Heather. "Heather is the medium."

Nina looked at Heather, the supposedly sane one.

Heather nodded. "I was born that way."

Nina looked expectantly at Lorna, wondering what craziness was going to come out of her mouth.

"Are you injured?" Lorna asked.

"Like..." Nina frowned. "You mean like in my brain?"

She did feel like she was in a dream. Or a 1900s asylum where all the patients escaped.

Lorna smiled kindly and shook her head. "No. Like anything physical that you can see? A cut? Bruise?"

Nina glanced down at her sneakers. Her feet throbbed from where she'd trampled the bottoms against the street.

"She was running around barefoot," Heather said.

"Yes, feet," Vivien said.

"Perfect. Take off your shoes." Lorna stood and moved toward Nina.

Heather sat and pulled off her work boots before tugging at her socks. Nina remained standing.

"May I hold your hand?" Lorna asked, reaching for her.

Nina frowned but didn't resist when the woman touched her. Vibrations moved up her arm and over her body until they reached her toes. Her feet began to tingle and grow warm. Heather reached for Lorna's other hand and propped up one of her feet so that the sole faced Nina.

The skin of Heather's feet began to redden, and a tiny cut formed near the arch. At the same time, the ache in Nina's foot lessened.

Nina snatched her hand away. "What is this? How are you doing that?"

Heather sat back and examined her new wounds. "Do we have antiseptic?"

"Medicine cabinet," Vivien answered.

Nina frowned in disbelief. She stepped on the back of her sneaker and pulled out her foot. Leaning against the door, she jerked off her sock. Her foot was completely healed. "I don't understand."

"I'm a healer," Lorna said. "And really good at locating lost things."

"So, you were all born, like, um, witches?" Nina wasn't sure what to call them.

"I was not born with these gifts," Lorna corrected. "They came to me several years ago after I arrived here, in Freewild Cove, and found a ring from Grandma Julia."

Nina dropped her foot and looked at the ring on her hand.

"Can't you feel it?" Lorna asked. "Even a little?"

"You should be able to sense it," Vivien said. "The tingling? An awareness that something is different inside you?"

Nina rubbed her hand. It buzzed as if electricity hummed through it.

"I'm not magical," Nina denied.

"Yet," Lorna said.

"I'm not a witch," Nina insisted.

"We don't exactly label what we are," Vivien said. "You can call it whatever you like."

"I don't have magical powers," Nina stated as clearly as she could, given the nerves running rampant through her body. She balled her hands into fists to stop the shaking. "I tried to move objects with my mind when I was little, but that was just goofing off. It never worked."

"It's different for everyone." Lorna kept her smile soft and soothing. "You see, I've always had caretaker tendencies with my family, but Julia's ring amplified that inside of me. Sue—"

"She's part of this?" Nina asked.

"She's a cleaner," Lorna said. "With a wave of her hand, the house looks like a team of pros attacked it for hours. She was always cleaning up and hiding other people's messes, so that's how her gift surfaced."

"I don't have anything like that." Nina wasn't sure why she was even entertaining this. It was nonsense, right? She looked at her foot again. "Unless being unlucky is magical? Because I am very unlucky."

"We'll find out," Vivien said.

"So, who's Julia? This is her ring?" Nina held up her hand.

"My grandmother," Heather said.

"You're sisters?" Nina frowned. Lorna had called Julia her grandma. "Cousins?"

"As good as," Vivien answered. "But legally, no. Everyone just calls her Grandma Julia."

"Julia passed away," Heather continued, "but you'll most likely meet her. The best we can explain it, she enchanted her rings to find the people who need them. So, whatever is happening in your life, we're here to help. You're not alone. We—"

Nina's phone began to ring. She looked around her feet, realizing she'd dropped her duffel bag on the floor when she walked in. She reached for it, pulling the phone out of a pocket.

"Oh, shit. Jacob." She reached for her purse and eyed the three women as she grabbed her sock and shoe. Carrying them, she left one foot bare as she

47

pulled open the door. "I can't do this now. I have some place to be."

"Jacob? Is he who you're scared of?" Vivien asked. "We can help. I promise it's nothing we haven't done before. Sue can tell you. We had to rid her of a doozy of an ex."

"No. Don't help. Jacob's..." Nina stepped outside onto the porch and hurried to her car. She didn't bother to finish explaining. Both feet felt amazing as if she'd had a pedicure and massage.

Getting behind the wheel, she glanced at the porch to see all three ladies staring at her. She answered the phone. "I'm on my way."

"I'll be here," Jacob said before she hung up on him.

Lorna gave her a small wave as Heather tried to usher the other two back inside. Vivien smiled sadly and nodded as if they shared a secret.

"Fucking crazy-ass town," Nina muttered. "Where the hell did I move to?"

CHAPTER SIX

Jacob had the most comforting brown eyes, deep and soulful, like they held the key to every woman's dream. Whenever she met him, they struck her as something different, something special. They promised safety.

Logically, she knew it was a psychological misfire that gave her romantic feelings and a fascination for his eyes. Transference, maybe? He had been the first one to make her feel safe after her ordeal. He hadn't pried, didn't hound her with questions like the police, doctors, and nurses. He merely talked to her, normally, until she had started to *feel* a little bit normal. After coming off the cocktail of whatever had been in her system, her first clear memory was of his eyes.

Now, they drew her from the other side of the coffee shop's glass door to where he sat in a back corner. Nina pushed her way inside.

The second she appeared, he stood. His curly brown hair was a little long. He might work with attorneys, but he didn't dress like a lawyer. In a room full of suits, he'd wear blue jeans and sunglasses pushed back on his head. Now he was in an open Hawaiian shirt with a bold blue flower print over a t-shirt. The sunglasses were on the table next to his phone.

Instantly the smell of coffee grounds surrounded her. These places always had the same kind of hipster-cool feel. Paintings bragging the names of local artists lined the wood-planked walls. Kiosks boasted homemade jams, soy candles, and merchandise with the shop's logo. Near the register were displays of handcrafted earrings and necklaces.

Though it was near closing time, people were still in deep conversations at the tables. Two men held hands as they leaned across a table to whisper to each other. If they weren't in love, they were well on their way to falling there. Their fingers danced together, twining and weaving as if the couple lived in their own world.

Four twenty-something girls had textbooks

spread out between them but seemed to have abandoned the pretense of studying for something on their phones. Three boys were trying very hard to get the girls' attention, much to the dismay of a group of businessmen at a nearby table. The men were heatedly pounding out the details of a contract they passed amongst themselves.

An older couple sat beside each other in a booth, both reading books. The woman reached over to pat her husband's arm without bothering to look up from her pages. Next to them, a man in a green army jacket shared a scone with a woman in a tight red dress.

"Nina." Jacob waved for her to join him at the small round table.

She had to weave through couples on dates to get to him. As she neared, he pulled out a chair for her. A plate filled with crumbs and two disposable coffee cups were on the table.

"I'm sorry it took me a while to get here." Nina thought about her healed feet as she sat down. She almost hoped she was crazy and hallucinating. The alternative was to believe her eyes, and that would be too strange. "It's been a weird day."

"Lots of cream, lots of sugar." Jacob slid one of the coffees toward her. His strong hands had calluses from hard work. He had a pleasant voice too, not all smooth and Lothario, but relaxed and thoughtful. "Town appears nice. A little small, but friendly. At least the coffee is good."

She couldn't help an ironic laugh. "I was going for a low crime rate."

"Does it make you feel safe?" he asked. "That's all that matters."

"I doubt that's why you're here." Nina fingered the cup but didn't drink from it. She traced her finger along the name and silently read, "*The Coffee Shop in Freewild Cove.*"

It was a long name for a business and too on the nose.

Jacob leaned in and said in a low tone, "I watched him make it, and it has not left my sight."

He never judged her for her fear.

When she didn't drink, he picked it up and lifted the lid. He poured some of the coffee into his nearly empty cup. He then took a long drink.

He popped the lid back on her cup and slid it toward her. "Little cold, but..."

"Thank you." Nina took a drink. "It is good coffee."

Jacob studied her for a moment. "Are you hungry?"

"No." She shook her head.

"Are you sure? I can be your royal taster if you like. The white chocolate scones are good."

Damn those kind eyes. She turned her attention to her hands on her cup. "I know it's eccentric."

"A stranger drugged you in a restaurant. I'd be worried if you weren't cautious after that. I'm cautious just hearing about it."

Nina looked up to see if he was serious.

He kept his gaze steady. "You're in here, Nina. You're trying to get on with your life. I call that a big win. Don't discount that. A year ago, you wouldn't have made it through the door."

Nina nodded that she'd heard him. "So, why are you here?"

"Maybe I missed your company." He tried to smile, but it didn't reach his eyes. He was worried about something.

Nina leaned forward and whispered, "Did they let him out? I thought he was denied bail. Did he escape? Tell me he's not out."

"He's not out. My contacts at the prison said all Teeter does is sit inside a cell and meditate when he's not saying creepy things to the other prisoners. If anything changes, they'll call."

Nina nodded. "My therapist thinks I should go

confront him in prison. He keeps trying to get me to go there. I don't want to."

"That doesn't sound like solid advice. Teeter is not your normal criminal. There isn't any remorse or explanations for what he's done." Jacob shook his head. "No. You'll confront him in court."

Nina had found the therapist's advice strange at the time. "So, what are you doing here?"

"Judge Briar was in a skiing accident last week. I'm told it was a complete freak thing. There was rock debris under the snow. No one is sure how it even got there since the resort keeps a close eye on the slopes. They think it might have been sabotaged by a disgruntled worker. Apparently, it resulted in a massive skier pileup. His Honor is in traction at a Swiss hospital. Judge Rapaport is presiding over the case now." Jacob reached across the table, holding her hand under his as if to keep her steady. "Teeter's lawyer requested a bail review with the new judge."

"What does that mean?"

"It means that his lawyer is right on schedule cementing his place in the lower levels of actual Hell. I hate that fame whore," Jacob muttered under his breath. "Sorry. You don't need my commentary."

Nina agreed with him about Teeter's attorney.

"No, you're right. Only a soulless, bloodsucking demon would defend the indefensible."

Jacob kept his hand on hers. His was the only contact that didn't make her want to jump out of her skin. She pulled away and put her hands in her lap. She didn't want to mistake his kindness and empathy for anything more.

"Really, though, Jacob, what does this mean? If you're here, then you're worried he'll get bail," Nina reasoned. She hated the fear that knotted inside of her. It had been there for so long that she couldn't remember what it felt like to live without it.

One of the boys began to whistle for the girls' attention. Nina suppressed her irritation at the loud noise and leaned forward.

"Judge Rapaport is new. I've watched him in court a few times." Jacob tapped his fingers on the table and then held his empty coffee cup. He tipped it back and forth as if distracting himself. "Honestly, in my opinion, he acts like he has a lot to prove, or maybe he feels the need to show off his knowledge. Either way, it's a sign of insecurity. He dawdles over case law, gets long-winded when stating his opinions, and..."

Jacob lifted and dropped the empty cup several

times, letting the hollow sound bounce off the tabletop.

"And is unpredictable?" she finished for him.

"Is a little too determined to show he's a free-thinker, which, yes, makes him unpredictable," Jacob answered. "I don't trust people who have too much to prove."

Nina sat back and glanced at a nearby table. Mr. Army Jacket had his arms crossed over his chest as the woman in red gestured wildly. The couple looked to be bickering. Suddenly, the man turned to her and glared in her direction.

Nina darted her gaze back to Jacob. "Thank you for never sugarcoating it. Delany would have just patted me on the head and told me not to worry."

"Delany is a good person and a hell of a district attorney, but I get what you mean. You deserve to be given things straight up. No bullshit. I promised you that much the first time we met."

"You remember that?" she asked in surprise. "Or do you say that to everyone when you first meet them?"

He gave her a strange look. "I remember every conversation we've ever had. Nina, you must know that I—"

"Well, I'm sorry, princess," Mr. Army Jacket

yelled at his girlfriend. The conversations around the coffee shop instantly stopped as people turned to watch the show. "Not all of us can afford a month-long cruise. If your mother wants us to get married on a ship so badly, maybe she should pay for it."

"Oh, so I'm unreasonable." The woman shot up in her chair, causing a loud scrape as it slid behind her. "But you could afford a brand-new pickup and to spend three weeks camping with the guys."

"I was logging. It's a job," he defended. "Maybe if you had one—"

"Hey, buddy, maybe you should take it outside," one of the businessmen stood up.

"Mind your own damn business," the woman in red snapped. She grabbed her half-eaten scone and threw it at him.

"Come on," Mr. Army Jacket hooked the woman around the waist and escorted her to the door. On his way out, he again glared at Nina. His eyes strayed a little too long.

When he finally looked away, Nina turned her attention back to Jacob. "I'm sorry, you were saying?"

"I came here because I wanted to—" he began.

"Nina?"

Nina's name caused her to stiffen and look around.

Sue made her way from near the front counter. "Hi! I thought that was you."

"Oh, ah..." Nina wasn't sure what to say. For a moment, she'd forgotten about the strange witch ladies and their supposed powers.

"Sue." Sue pointed at herself as she came to a stop near the table.

"I remember," Nina quickly responded. "Um, Sue, this is a friend of mine, Jacob. Jacob, Sue. Her boyfriend runs the shop."

"That he does," Sue said.

"Tell him he has great coffee," Jacob said.

"That I will." Sue smiled as she hovered near them. "Jameson is in the back if you are interested in that job. I told him all about you."

"Um..." Nina tried to think of a polite answer.

"You're looking for a job?" Jacob asked.

"Well, I..." Nina shrugged. "Not really?"

But maybe she should have been.

"Oh." Sue's smile dropped some. "No worries. It was just a thought."

"Did something happen with the school district?" Jacob asked, lowering his voice as if that would keep his inquiry private.

"Oh, are you a teacher?" Sue asked, her smile returning.

"Bus driver," Nina answered. "Or I was."

Sue looked as if she wanted to ask more, but Nina didn't feel like explaining what happened. If she did that, she'd have to explain why, and the why always led back to the same horror.

"Nina, are you...?" Jacob looked at Sue and didn't finish his question.

"Do you work around here, Jacob?" Sue asked, still hovering.

"I'm a private investigator. We tend to work everywhere." Jacob easily slid into conversations. His safe eyes turned their attention onto Sue, and his soothing voice directed itself toward her.

Nina found herself getting a little jealous, though it served to remind her that she couldn't read into Jacob's kindness.

"How intriguing." Sue looked as if she wanted to sit down with them but refrained. "Are you here about the phrog?" She turned her gaze to Nina. "Lorna called me and told me what happened. Terrifying. I was about to head over to the rental house to help pack up your things, so you don't have to go back."

"*She's a cleaner,*" Lorna had said about Sue. "*With a wave of her hand, the house looks like a team of pros attacked it for hours.*"

Nina looked at Sue's hand. The woman wore an antique ring. The jewelry on Nina's finger began to vibrate again, sending the strange buzzing sensation up her arm. She really wanted it to stop.

"Yeah, you were saying something about having frogs earlier." Jacob frowned.

When his attention was turned, Sue glanced meaningfully to indicate Jacob and mouthed, "Are you okay?"

Nina gave a slight nod, realizing the woman was worried about her, and that was why she was hovering.

"Is there a reptile infestation in your new place?" Jacob asked. "I've heard of that happening. Frogs sometimes come inside houses to escape the more extreme temperatures. Are they checking for leaks? They like damp—"

"Phrog with a P H," Nina corrected. "There was a squatter staying in the attic who didn't move out when I moved in."

"Are you all right?" Jacob reached across the table to grab her hand. "Did they do something?"

"Scared me is all." Nina again pulled away from him and put her hands in her lap. "I'm fine. The landlord let me out of the lease."

"He better," Jacob stated. "You let me know if you have any trouble."

"*She's* been good about it," Nina assured him, glancing at Sue. "I don't think she could have known someone was up there. Heather has offered to let me stay in her guest room until another one of her rentals opens up."

"Will you be comfortable there?" Jacob asked. "I mean, I'm hardly at home if you need a place to stay. No one will know you're there. You're welcome to—"

"No, thank you," Nina denied. That was the last thing her libido needed, fuel on the fire of her crush. "I don't want to move back there. Not right now."

"Yeah, sure." Jacob almost looked disappointed. "Offer stands, though."

"Well, I guess I'll see you over at Heather's later." Sue slowly backed away as no one invited her to stay.

Nina nodded.

"And don't you worry about anything," she said. "I'll make sure your belongings make it to you safe and sound."

"Thank you." Nina twisted the ring on her finger, tugging it lightly to test whether she could take it off.

When Sue left, Jacob prompted, "A phrog?"

Nina shrugged. "That's what the police called it."

"And you don't know who it was?"

She shook her head. "They seem to think it's a vagrant. He was there before me, so it doesn't have anything to do with me. Just like that bike messenger who knocked me over and sprained my ankle. Or that girl who robbed the convenience store seconds after I left it and caused an eyewitness to mistakenly point me out as the culprit. The grocery store sushi gave me food poisoning. The truck that hit my parked bus. It's just more bad luck, I guess."

"I knew about the messenger, the robbery, and the sushi. But a truck hit the school bus? Was anyone hurt? Is that why you need a job?" Jacob frowned as a group of guys walked by their table.

Nina waited for them to pass before saying, "No, the kids weren't in it. I'd already dropped them off for a field trip. There wasn't any good bus parking at the museum, so I had to find a place along the road. A flower delivery truck t-boned it. A minute earlier and I would have been inside. The school board wasn't happy about it, but they didn't fire me, though they did say that technically it was my responsibility to take care of the bus while it was in my possession. It was recommended I take a leave of absence to

*—how did Superintendent Sherry put it?—*to refind my center."

"Is refind even a word?" Jacob asked.

"Maybe? Sherry used it." Nina waved her hand in dismissal. She pushed up from the table. "Anyway, I can't blame her. With the way my luck has been going, I shouldn't be responsible for the lives of children."

"Normally, I would say I don't believe in luck." Jacob also stood. "But in your case..."

Unlucky number seven.

"Yeah." Nina sighed. "One of the therapists I talked to said that when people go through trauma, something inside them changes, like we all have this invisible electrical pulse we send out to others, and it gets altered. And if the signal isn't fixed, it can often lead to re-victimization. Maybe my signal attracts chaos."

She didn't believe that. Not really. Nina often thought that by escaping death, she'd somehow cheated fate. The accident, the robber, the food poisoning, the bus, the home intruder...they were all just death coming to finish the job and right some cosmic imbalance her life caused.

Jacob came around the table and very sternly stated, "None of it is your fault."

"It's getting late. I should get back to the house." Nina started going toward the door, slow enough so that he could easily walk with her. They wove past a few of the tables. "Thank you for coming to tell me about the bail hearing. You'll let me know when you know more?"

"Always." He held open the door for her and then followed her outside. The streetlights had turned on, and the soft yellow glow illuminated the quiet street. "But I didn't just come to tell you about the hearing."

"Are you worried I won't come back to testify?" Nina put her hand on his arm. The warmth of him curled around her fingers. She knew she should pull away but couldn't force her hand to obey. "I promise I'll be there. I know how important it is. Believe me. I just can't have people asking me about it. That reporter... I don't want to talk to the press. Delany said she'd keep my name as a Jane Doe."

"I came for you," he said.

"For me what?"

"Just you. I wanted to see you."

It felt as if he inched closer, but she couldn't be sure. Her hand flexed against his arm as she tried to let go.

"Nina, I think you know. I mean, you must know I like you."

"I like you, too, Jacob." She finally managed to release him.

He stopped her from backing away by taking hold of her shoulder. "I mean, I man-woman like you."

"Oh," she whispered before adding a much louder, "*oh!,*" as she realized what he meant.

"Yes. Oh." He chuckled, nodding. "Please tell me I'm not imagining..."

"I, you, but..." Nina tried to calm her whirling mind. Was this conversation happening? Now? "No."

"No?" He released her shoulder and stepped back.

"Not imagining," she said. "Just surprised you said it. You did say you liked-liked me, right? I mean, can we even do that? Isn't there a rule against it? Conflict of interest? You're working on the case, and I'm part of the case, and you have to be impartial in your investigation, and this is all very confusing."

"I'll be staying at the hotel for a few days," he said. "How about for now, I walk you to your car, and you can call me later after you've had a moment to think, and it's less confusing."

She nodded for lack of a better suggestion and took a step toward where she'd parked while keeping her attention focused fully on him.

"And for the record, lawyers becoming romantically involved with their clients is unethical and pretty much a no-no, but there is no proscription barring an investigator from asking a witness on a date. So, we're good, if you want us to be good."

"Okay, so we're good." Nina smiled, feeling a little giddy. "I'll think and then call you."

Jacob glanced down the street. "I thought you drove here. Do you need a ride?"

"I did drive." Nina pointed. "I'm right—"

She gasped to find an empty parking spot and turned to look along the few vehicles that were there.

"No. No-no-no-no-no." Nina went to where her car was last seen. "I was parked right here."

"Someone stole your car?" Jacob frowned, pulling out his cell phone. "We have to report this."

"No. No. No." Nina hit her hand against her hip. Her keys were in her pocket. "I think my purse was in there. My wallet. My phone. Dammit. This can't be happening."

She sat down on the curb and put her head in her hands. Her thoughts raced as she barely registered

Jacob pacing behind her as he talked to the police dispatcher.

Nina wanted to scream. She wanted to laugh. She wanted to walk out into traffic.

Her eyes went to a set of headlights coming down the street. The car was only doing about fifteen miles per hour. She doubted it would do much damage. With the way her luck was going, she'd end up with a broken hip and months of painful recovery.

This was not how she imagined her midlife.

This was not how she imagined *any* part of life.

"They're on their way." Jacob sat down next to her.

Nina put her head back into her hands.

Jacob put his arm around her shoulders. "It's going to be all right. I promise. I'll stay with you until this is handled or however long you need."

CHAPTER SEVEN

THE CRACK TEAM from the Freewild Cove Police Department wasted two hours taking Nina's report. Most of which was spent between repeatedly asking if anyone she knew might have borrowed it and was she sure? And wasn't she the lady who had the phrog in the attic? Then they declared that this kind of thing rarely happens, and it was probably just some joyriding kids who watched videos on social media telling them how to steal a car with a phone charger. Apparently, car theft by phone charger was a West Coast big-city problem nowadays, and big-city problems always trickled out to small towns.

In the end, they promised to investigate it and keep her informed. They suggested she cancel her phone and credit cards and report it to her insurance.

Beyond that, there wasn't much she could do, but if she wanted a copy of their report, it would be ready by noon the next day, and she could come pick it up at the police department.

Nina frowned. She watched the cruiser's tail-lights as they followed in Jacob's car. "Thank you for your help. If you weren't here to vouch for me, I'm sure they would have arrested me for making a false report or something. They couldn't seem to believe I'd have two legal incidences in one day. Not in their perfect town."

"I got the impression they were both new," he answered. "Don't worry. At the very least, they should know how to write a report. That's all you'll need for your insurance."

Don't worry, unlucky number seven.

That was easier said than done. Her mind swirled with mounting stress. She would have to pray the value of her car was enough to pay off the title loan she took out on it...and that insurance would cover it. Then what? How was she supposed to buy a new car while taking a leave from work? Not to mention a down payment? Did this town even have public transportation?

Nina watched the police cruiser turn. She knew they weren't going to help her. Eventually, she'd end up in some database that listed people who filed too many reports. Like Old Lady Beatrice, who lived down the street from where Nina grew up. She used to call the cops for everything—kids lurking in the bushes smoking cigarettes (incorrigible deviants up to no good, naturally); the lawn boy not cutting her grass short enough, so he'd have to come back sooner (thievery, of course); some guy in the park who looked at her funny (potential rapist). The list went on and on.

"I don't want to be known as the new Beatrice," Nina muttered.

"I'm sorry?" Jacob asked in confusion.

"Never mind. Ignore me. It's been a long day." She pointed the way toward Heather's house. "Turn up here."

Jacob did as she instructed.

"I was thinking I'd stay in town for a few days," Jacob said.

"You mentioned that." Nina turned her full attention to him, watching him drive.

"How about I pick you up tomorrow around noon and give you a ride to the police station?"

Nina nodded. "That would be great, thank you."

"And after, maybe we can grab lunch?" He glanced at her and smiled.

Nina instantly thought of her missing wallet.

"My treat," he said.

"Yeah, sure, thanks. That'd be great as well."

Nina felt like a hot mess. She wanted to ask him why he was being so nice to her or why he even claimed to like her but refrained. She had very few people she trusted and wasn't about to start questioning Jacob's motives now.

They rode in relative silence as she directed him to the house. When he pulled into the drive, she watched as lights flipped on in one of the upper-story windows. A shadow crossed as someone moved inside.

"Thank you for everything," she said, reaching for the door.

His hand moved to capture hers. He held it for a few seconds before letting go. "I'll see you tomorrow."

Her hand lingered, still feeling his touch. She took a deep breath. "Tomorrow."

Nina got out of the car and watched him pull away. She reminded herself that in the whole mess that was her life, Jacob's friendship was the one good thing she could believe in. She shouldn't question him or his motives. What he saw in her, she had no idea.

Pre-Teeter, she wouldn't have questioned her worth. She had been fabulous, and she'd owned it. Now...not so much. Teeter had taken more than time from her.

As Jacob drove down the street and the taillights disappeared into the darkness, she turned her attention to the house. She debated on whether to go inside or just find a nice park bench to sleep on. Surely people camped out on the beach.

"And the tide would probably drag me out to sea," she muttered. It wouldn't kill her, but she might lose a foot to a shark.

Another shadow moved across the upstairs window.

"I have nothing, and I'm staying in a house full of witches. Sure. Why not? This is my life," she whispered dryly. As she said it, her hand tingled. She tugged at the ring, trying to yank it off. The tight jewelry didn't budge. "And my finger will probably fall off in the middle of the night."

Nina made her way to the porch and lifted her hand to knock. The door opened before she could touch it. She waited to see who answered. No one was there.

"Heather?" she asked, poking her head inside. "Hello? It's Nina."

She started to close the door without going in so she could knock properly.

"Nina?" Lorna appeared from the dining room. "I thought I heard your voice. Come in. Come in." The woman waved her forward. "Did you eat? I can whip something up for you if you like."

"I'm good, thank you," Nina answered.

"I'm going to heat up some pasta, just in case you change your mind." Lorna moved to go back to where she came from. "Shrimp fettuccini Alfredo all right? I have a new pasta maker, and I'm obsessed."

"Wait."

Lorna paused expectantly. "I have marinara, too, if you prefer."

Nina stared at Lorna for a moment. "Can I ask you—?"

"Yes, please. Anything." Lorna nodded. "I'm glad you came back. I was worried we might have sprung too much on you too soon. Learning that the paranormal is real can be a lot to digest."

"What did you mean when you said you were a finder?" Nina asked.

"Oh." Lorna seemed surprised by the question. "I have a knack for finding lost things. It manifested from my having three kids. Moms always get asked where everything is."

"So, not magic? Just a good memory."

"Oh, no, it's magical. I can find things that I've never seen before." Lorna came a little closer. She moved as if she had drunk too much coffee and was in the midst of a caffeine buzz. "Like, once, I found this old tome of a book that held all of Julia's séance records and spells. It is like a grimoire if you've heard of those. Anyway, it was underneath the stage in the old theater Julia had built like a hundred years ago, in this secret-compartment trap door that no one knew was there. It's where we learned to conduct seances to talk to people beyond the grave. We'll show it to you later. It could help you with whatever is happening."

"Could you, say, find a missing car?"

"Sure, if we forget where we parked," Lorna said. "It's happened a few times at the mall."

"What if the car was stolen?"

Lorna frowned. "Nina, was your car stolen?"

Nina nodded. "Outside the coffee shop tonight. My phone and wallet were in there too. The police didn't seem too hopeful about getting it back unless some joyriding kids happen to abandon it somewhere —not that they know for sure it was kids."

"I'll grab my keys." Lorna took the steps two at a time and disappeared up the stairs. Nina heard the woman calling Vivien and Heather to join them.

"She's...crime magnet," Heather's voice drifted down.

"Strange..." Vivien answered, the words muffled.

Nina crept closer to the stairs to listen.

"Is that what we think this is? A haunting?" Lorna asked. "Can ghosts steal cars?"

"I've heard of phantom drivers," Heather said. "But they usually manifest their cars with them."

"Possessed car?" Vivien suggested. "Like that Stephen King movie? But that doesn't explain the creeper in the attic."

Nina craned her neck to hear better.

"Possessed human?" Vivien put forth. "I mean, it must be supernatural, right? We're thinking super-natural."

"Two crimes in one day. That's an awful coinci-dence," Lorna said. "It has to be why she's here. We have to help her."

"She did say she was unlucky and—" Heather's words were cut off by the heavy sound of footsteps on the stairs.

Nina backtracked to the door to pretend like she'd been waiting the entire time. Vivien led the way downstairs. Her hair was pulled onto the top of her head, and she'd removed her makeup for the night. The pajama pants and t-shirt indicated she'd been about to go to bed. Lorna and Heather followed, both looking as they had earlier.

"Tough luck," Vivien said. Her fluffy slippers swished against the floor as she shuffled her feet. "Don't worry. Lorna can find your car. I think the only thing she can't find is the virginity I lost back in high school."

"Classy," Heather muttered with a small laugh.

"It's not like I want it back." Vivien chuckled.

"Yeah, please, never ask me to look for that," Lorna teased.

"The police think it might be teenagers joyriding," Nina explained to get them focused on her car. The stress kept building as if each second was one closer to someone setting the vehicle on fire to hide evidence.

"Maybe." Vivien suppressed a yawn.

"Sorry for the inconvenience. I can see you were going to bed. Thank you for being willing to do this tonight." Though Nina really wanted to find her car, she couldn't expect them to drop everything for her. "I know my problems do not constitute an emergency for everyone else."

Vivien waved her hand in dismissal. "Ignore me. I took an allergy pill. They make me sleepy."

"Sooner we find it, the better." Lorna held her car keys in her hand and walked out the door.

As they moved toward one of the cars parked in the driveway, Lorna stood on the lawn. She tilted her head back and closed her eyes as if sensing her environment. Nina felt a shiver work over her body and her scalp tingled.

"I'll drive," Lorna said, prompting Heather out of the driver's seat. Heather climbed in the back next to Vivien.

Nina sat beside Lorna. The woman pulled out of the driveway. No one spoke as they drove slowly down the street and stopped at a crossing. Vivien rested her head against a window and closed her eyes. Heather searched their surroundings without appearing to look too hard.

"I could use some help," Lorna said.

Vivien reached forward from the backseat and touched Lorna's shoulder. Heather grabbed hold of Vivien's arm.

Once connected, Lorna whispered, "Got it."

Vivien and Heather let go and settled back. The car sped as Lorna took them across town, past closed businesses, and dark houses, until the streetlights spread farther apart. The moon didn't shine too brightly, which created shadowed paths between dots of light. Lorna slowed the car a few times, and the other women automatically touched her, seeming to prompt where she might search next.

Nina wasn't sure what she'd expected as they drove along the beach. Lorna's finder power felt more like they hoped to get lucky by driving aimlessly around town.

The dark ocean stretched into the distance. Heather rolled her window down, and the sound of waves drifted in. Lorna pulled over near a picnic table and hopped out of the car.

Nina frowned and opened her door. There were no other vehicles in sight.

"You're saying they drove it into the ocean?" Even as Nina looked for tire tracks in the sand, she didn't expect to find any.

Lorna went toward a trash can and grimaced as she leaned over the side. She held her breath as she turned her face away from the bin to reach in.

"Lorna, no," Vivien scolded, not getting out of the car. "Gross."

Lorna retrieved something from the bin and dropped it on the table. Nina joined her, surprised to find her purse half-covered in what she hoped was a milkshake.

"How did you...?" Pinching the clean parts, Nina opened it and managed to dump out her wallet, phone, face powder, and lip gloss. A strange smell came from the purse, so she tossed it back into the trash bin and only kept the contents. She checked her wallet. "It's all here. Even the cash. I mean it's only five dollars, but still. I don't understand. Why?"

She proceeded to turn around and search for signs of her car.

"Your car's not here," Lorna answered without being asked as she headed back toward the vehicle. "This was just stop one on the mystery van tour."

"Mystery Machine," Heather corrected. She leaned into the passenger window and retrieved hand sanitizer from the glove box.

Lorna held up her hands while Heather squirted liquid on them. "Thanks, Mr. Smithers."

"Hey, I'm Scooby," Heather corrected. "The brains behind this operation."

"Let's go. I'm getting hungry," Vivien said.

Nina scooped up her belongings and hurried to get into the vehicle. When Heather handed her the hand sanitizer, she didn't use it. She couldn't take the smell of rubbing alcohol.

Lorna started driving the way they came, winding along the beach. Nina opened her internet search and pulled the screen down to refresh.

"Captured Serial Killer. Robert Chester Teeter arrested and held without bail..."

Nina took a steadying breath and shut off the screen.

"Phone good?" Heather asked.

"Yeah." Nina nodded. "Still works."

"Ladies, I could use a little more help," Lorna said as she drove. Heather and Vivien reached forward to touch her.

Nina slowly lifted her hand. "Should I...?"

"Definitely," Heather answered. "It'll help."

Nina hesitated before reaching over to touch Lorna's forearm. A shock of energy rushed through her, lifting her hair around her head. The same thing happened to Lorna as strands of the woman's hair lifted with a static charge and touched the cloth ceiling. The engine revved as they sped up.

Nina felt a mix of emotions wash over her—concern, excitement, determination. The strangest part was that she didn't think the feelings came from inside her. They flowed from where she touched Lorna. Nina's emotions were pure stress, a giant ball of it amplified by the constant fear.

"Come on, baby, where are you?" Lorna whispered. "Come on. You can't hide from me. I'm gonna find you."

Lorna turned off onto a country road and drove faster. Dust flew behind the car, and Nina heard the occasional thud of rocks kicking up from the tires and hitting the side panels.

They turned several more times down seemingly abandoned roads. Trees appeared to reach for them as they passed. The car bounced over dried ruts in the dirt road, lifting Nina from her seat. The farther they drove, the more ominous their surroundings became. The headlights became the only light source as they moved through the woods. She saw the faint shape of a derelict cabin fly past the window.

"I have my wallet and phone," Nina said, trying hard to keep her fear in check. This area was too isolated. "Maybe we should turn around."

"It does kind of look like the beginning sequence of a movie where things are about to go bad," Heather agreed. A streak of lightning flashed as if to prove her point, illuminating the trees and causing their branches to look like hands stretching toward them.

"Keep going," Vivien stated.

"Oh, this thief is not winning." Lorna leaned

forward in determination. "I know your car is close. I can feel it."

"What if the thief is still out here?" Nina reasoned. "It's not worth risking our lives for a car. We know about where it is. We can tell the cops, and they can come get it in the morning."

Another streak of lightning flashed, but there was no rain.

Vivien gave a small laugh. "Don't worry. We can handle anything that comes at us."

Nina wanted to point out how cocky that sounded. She had been brave like that once before someone came along and pointed out her true vulnerability. Now bravery felt like foolishness.

She thought of the constant panic in her chest and realized her fear wasn't as intense as it should have been.

Lorna slammed on the brakes and jerked the car to the side so that the back tires slid on the gravel. She pointed the high beams at Nina's car as it idled in a ditch between two trees. She laid on the horn. One figure suddenly became two as a couple parted in the backseat. A light sheen fogged the windows.

Vivien laughed. "Ha! Ultimate cockblock."

Heather hopped out the back and gave a gruff

yell, "Hey! Get out of the car slowly with your hands up."

The back door opened, and a half-naked woman darted into the trees clutching her red dress to her chest.

"She was at the coffee shop," Nina said, recognizing the thief.

Sure enough, naked Mr. Army Jacket followed behind his girlfriend. He practically dove out of the car into the trees. They could hear him scrambling through the underbrush to escape, yelping as something unfortunate apparently happened in his unclothed state. The woman screamed at him to hurry.

Vivien laughed harder.

Lorna rapidly beeped the horn.

"Hey," Heather belted again. "Get back here!"

"Well, that was worth waking up for," Vivien said.

"Let's go," Lorna ordered. "No reason to hang out on a creepy road in the middle of the night with criminals about."

"I can't believe they stole my car to make out." Nina approached the vehicle cautiously. The fog had begun to clear from the windows.

"That is gross," Heather agreed, slamming the

back door shut. "We'll have Sue detail it for you." She motioned her hand to encompass the back. "She'll get all the criminal sex juice out of the upholstery."

The lingering smell of cologne added a sharp punctuation to Heather's comment as the woman got into the passenger seat. Nina hesitated before joining her inside. The engine continued to run.

"I will never be able to get the term sex juice out of my head." Nina tried not to gag as she looked at the backseat.

Heather laughed. "Sorry."

At least the front appeared clean except for some dirt on the floor mats. However, the steering column was cracked, and wires hung from the side.

"What the fuck?" Nina frowned. What was she supposed to do with a hot-wired car? The thing was already old, with hundreds of thousands of miles on it. Fixing it would cost more than it was worth.

"Drive back to the house. We'll see if Sue can do anything about that tomorrow. It's a mess. Maybe she can clean it. If not, we'll get a mechanic to come over to look at it and put in a new ignition switch." Heather turned to look back at Lorna. The bright lights still shown on them. She waved her hand and then pointed that Lorna should turn around so they could leave. "My knowledge of car thievery is pretty thin, but I think once you shut off the engine in a hot-wired car, we're not going to be able to get it running again until it's repaired."

Nina took a deep breath, not even wanting to consider how much the repairs might cost. "I'd never heard that, but then I've never dealt with this kind of thing before."

"Not all of my high school boyfriends were good ideas," Heather admitted before changing the subject back to Nina's problems. "Did that look like the same guy who was in the attic?"

"No. I don't think so. He was just someone from the coffee shop." Nina tried to navigate the car out of the ditch. The tires spun before finally catching. They lurched up the small incline onto the road. "He was arguing with his girlfriend and then with some of the other customers. We didn't say anything to each other. He glared at me, but he glared at everyone."

"That's really..." Heather frowned.

"Unlucky?" Nina offered. "Yep. Story of my life these days."

Heather nodded. "How long has your bad luck been going on?"

"Little over sixteen months." Nina followed

Lorna, trying to keep an eye on the hanging wires near her steering column.

"What happened sixteen months ago?" she asked.

"I don't want to talk about it." Nina gripped the wheel. She didn't even want to *think* about it. Especially when driving through the backwoods that time forgot with a creeper cabin and naked car-thieving hoodlums on the loose.

Heather looked out the window for a long moment before saying, "I'm sorry for what you went through. From what I was able to feel, it must have been horrible."

What she was able to feel? The woman said it like she *knew* the truth. She thought of the rush of emotions she'd experienced when she touched Lorna.

"I've just been worried about finding my car," Nina lied. "Money has been tight."

"When we were looking for your car, we could feel your emotions. Is your chest always that tight? Lorna mentioned it after she healed your feet, and it was still there tonight. She's worried you're going to have a stroke. Your blood pressure is too high."

Nina didn't answer. She wasn't sure what to say.

"Please, talk to me. What other unlucky things have been happening?"

Nina turned a corner, intently watching Lorna's taillights for the way back. "Some of my accounts were hacked. The bank caught the suspicious transactions and stopped them, but it took weeks for my new bank card to come in the mail. A bike messenger knocked me over. Stores shut early when I really need something. Traffic always sucks, and I'll sometimes get trapped in jams for hours, especially if I'm in a hurry. I've been pulled over multiple times for fitting some description. A woman accosted me in a store, convinced I was sleeping with her boyfriend, though I had no clue who he was or why he told her that. For a week, I was woken up hourly by prank calls—even when I changed my number. Things like that."

"And it's always initiated by someone else?" Heather asked.

"Are you asking if I bring it on myself?"

"No. I mean, the bad luck always stems from another person's actions—someone hacks you, someone trips you, someone pulls you over. The sequence of events starts with them."

"I suppose so."

"Did someone around you die before this all started?"

Nina stiffened and slowly nodded.

"Is it possible that person is angry with you?"

Her hands shook, and she managed another nod. "They could be."

"They?" Heather prompted.

Nina knew the woman was trying to get to the truth, but what could she say? How could she explain? She couldn't even get the words out to her therapist.

"What happened?" Heather insisted. "What do they think you did?"

"I survived." Nina pushed on the gas, closing the distance between her car and Lorna's. She wanted the ride to be over. It felt as if the past was nipping on her heels. The knot in her chest hardened, and it became difficult to breathe.

"Hey, easy." Heather touched her arm. Calming energy washed over her. "We're going to figure this out. I promise. You're not alone. We've dealt with ghost threats before. We always work it out. Things will get better."

Nina didn't want to ask Heather to explain her statement. The idea that the dead were somehow causing her bad luck was almost more terrifying than what had happened.

Well, no. That was a lie. Nothing was more terrifying than what had happened.

She reminded herself that Teeter was in prison. That was real. Jacob had assured her he was locked up tight. That was a tangible outcome based in reality. The bad guy was behind bars and couldn't hurt her.

But haunted bad luck? How did someone fight angry ghosts?

Nina leaned forward and continued to stare at Lorna's bumper as they neared town. Seeing streetlights caused her to feel more at ease. They were out of the woods, away from the horror movie loner cabin. "I don't want to talk anymore. I'm tired. I just want this day to be over."

Day? Try week, year, life.

Nina wanted a life do-over.

"Fair enough. It's been an unusual one." Heather agreed. "We can discuss this problem in the morning and devise a plan of action."

CHAPTER EIGHT

Nina awoke in a panic, trying to reason where she was trapped. Screams echoed around her, faint as they broke through from the past as a tormented memory. A medicinal smell lingered as if it permeated from her nightmares. She hated the smell of sanitizer and rubbing alcohol. A chill ran up her body as she remembered the cold metal slab she'd been on.

Nina's heart hammered violently, pounding so hard it choked her throat. She tried to sit up but couldn't move her limbs as she lay paralyzed. The strange room wasn't familiar. White walls looked too clean. Nothing felt right. Dark blue curtains cut through the white, giving her something to focus on.

Loud thumps sounded, and she tried to cry out,

but her tight throat only wheezed. The door crashed open as if breaking through her paralysis. She shot up in bed, grabbing her neck as she rasped for breath. The metal faded into a mattress, and the smell of flowers overcame the rubbing alcohol.

"Nina?" Vivien darted toward the bed. She pressed her knee into the mattress and reached for her. "What is it?"

Nina jerked back before the woman could touch her.

Vivien. Vivien was here. That meant she was in the Old Anderson House where Heather lived.

"Nina?" Vivien insisted. "Who is he? Talk to me."

Nina took several deep breaths, even when she no longer needed them, to keep from having to answer.

Very few people knew the meaning of real fear. They flirted with it. They watched documentaries that made them feel happy that they were safe in their homes as the danger lurked far, far away from their comfy couches. The world had become obsessed with deconstructing serial killers. And they always had stupid titles, like...

The Doctor's Plaything: Inside the sick lair of

Robert Chester Teeter, as told by the one woman who survived his operating table.

Fuck that shit. Nina refused to become another one of those tabloid stories for people's sick entertainment.

"Teeter?" Vivien narrowed her gaze as she stared at Nina. "Who's Teeter?"

"I didn't say anything," Nina protested in a whisper. She shook her head as if that one word could evoke him.

Teeter.

"Why do I keep hearing Teeter?" Vivien insisted.

Get out of my brain!

Nina leaned back, trying to put distance between them.

"Teeter?" Lorna appeared in the doorway. The color visibly drained from her face. "The serial killer? Robert Something Teeter. You know about that, Viv. They caught him recently about an hour or so north of here in Sallyville."

"That wannabe play doctor guy?" Vivien stiffened. "Is that who we're up against?"

"No," Nina whispered, not wanting to talk about it. She wanted it all to go away.

"Yes," Vivien countered, pressing her fist to her

chest. "Oh, sweetheart, I'm so sorry. We had no idea it was that bad."

"Okay. We can do this. We're fighting the ghost of a serial killer?" Lorna sat beside Vivien, turning sideways to face Nina. "I didn't realize he was dead."

"He's not. He's awaiting trial," Nina answered. "They caught him."

"Do you think that's who is outside in the...?" Lorna turned toward the window in a panic.

Vivien darted to look out the window. "Heather's out there."

Nina found herself compelled to look. She hurried to the window and peered down at the front lawn from the second story. "Where?"

Her hands shook, and she wasn't sure what she would do if he were out.

Vivien pointed behind her as she ran from the room, not giving a clear indication of where she meant.

Nina found Jacob's car parked in the street. Heather stood outside talking to him. Her arms defensively crossed over her chest.

"No." Nina sighed with relief. "That's Jacob. He's a friend."

Vivien was already down the stairs.

Nina heard the front door slam open. She rushed

after Vivien, taking the steps two at a time before leaping down the last bit of the way onto the living room floor. She darted through the open front door. As her bare feet moved from the wood of the porch to the concrete sidewalk, she stumbled. The texture sent a shockwave over her, making the world very closed and small as her peripheral vision dimmed. The yard disappeared into concrete. She remembered a flash of bright lights from around a corner.

"Nina." Jacob's voice sounded far away.

She saw movement advancing toward her, and her knees weakened. She swung her hands to block whatever was coming. Before she fell to the ground, strong arms grabbed hold.

"Hey, I got you," Jacob soothed.

"What's going on?" Heather demanded. "Let her go."

"No, it's all right," Vivien put forth. "She knows him. He relaxes her."

"Nina?" Jacob whispered, brushing back her hair from her cheek. "Can you hear me?"

"I'm all right. I...dizzy," she managed.

"You're shaking." Jacob's words sounded more like an accusation. He lifted her off her feet.

Nina would have protested if she could form a coherent sentence. Her vision swam between reality and memory. Jacob made her feel safe, but that contrasted with the memory of being carried. Her mind flashed back to crumbling concrete walls with chipped red paint. The damp musk became overpowered by the acrid smell of chemical sanitizer.

"Inside," Lorna ordered, bringing Nina back from the brink of unconsciousness.

Jacob carried her up the porch stairs. Before long, she was sitting on the couch with all four of them staring at her. Her mind slowly cleared as she focused on the room. Boxes of her belongings were stacked near the stairwell as if she'd never unpacked at the other house. She vaguely remembered seeing them the night before when they returned from finding her car.

"Nina?" Jacob sat next to her.

"I'm fine," she assured him. "Low blood sugar."

Vivien coughed and then arched a brow at Nina to indicate she knew the woman lied. She took a seat across from them.

"I'm fine," Nina repeated, steadying herself.

"So, Jacob. What were you doing here?" Vivien smiled as if she already knew the answer.

"I came to give Nina a ride to the police station to pick up a copy of the theft report," he answered. "But I see you found your car. Did the police bring it?"

Nina shook her head in denial. "Lorna found it for me."

"Sure. He's here about the car." Vivien started to laugh, but Heather knocked her on the shoulder. "What?"

"I should probably call the cops and tell them we found it." Nina tried to remember where she'd put her phone. After they made it back to the house, she'd been so tired she could barely make it up the stairs. Most likely, it was by the bed. She usually checked for news updates before going to sleep and when first waking up.

"Hey, Viv, why don't you help me with break-fast," Lorna suggested, leading the way to the kitchen. "Don't worry, Nina, I'll make it fast. We'll take care of that blood sugar."

"Good idea." Heather pulled Vivien up by the arm.

"It's not like I was going to say outright that they were meant to be together," Vivien protested, "but it's rather obvious."

"Ignore her," Heather said as she escorted Vivien from the room. "We're trying to get her help for the blurting."

Nina soon found herself alone with Jacob. He sat close to her on the couch.

"Interesting friends you have," he said. "Have you all known each other long?"

"Heather is—*was*—my landlord. The others I met yesterday." Nina tried artfully to move away from him as she adjusted in her seat. She became aware of the fact that she'd literally just jumped out of bed and wore an old t-shirt and yoga pants. She tried to push her hair away from her face, attempting to smooth what was happening with the mess.

"What really happened out there just now?" he asked.

"When I felt the sidewalk under my feet, I started flashing back to..." Nina frowned. "It's like someone was putting thoughts in my head, and for a moment, I couldn't tell the difference between now and then. I don't want to talk about it."

"You say you don't want to talk about things often." Jacob kept his voice soft and didn't appear to be judging her. "Maybe if you tried, you'd feel better. Don't hold everything in."

"I don't see how. It's not helpful to anyone. I remembered the concrete tunnel," Nina said. "There was red graffiti on the walls like someone had spray painted the number seven with angel wings. I was drugged. It's like all the other memories, scattered, hazy flashbacks. They're hardly worth mentioning. They won't help the case."

"You know I'm not here because of the case," Jacob stated as if the fact should be obvious. "I told you that I man-woman like you. I want you to talk about it because I think it will help you move past the trauma."

Nina started to answer, but Lorna returned holding a muffin.

"Eat this," Lorna ordered. "It's blueberry. It will help with the blood sugar, among other things."

"What other things?" Nina started reaching for the muffin. Her natural instinct was to not take food she didn't see prepared.

"Oh, antioxidants, and they prevent psychic attacks, things like that." Lorna gave a nervous chuckle to downplay the comment, but Nina knew from what she'd seen with the women that it wasn't a joke.

To her surprise, Jacob nodded. "I've heard that. My grandma used to claim something similar. Only she said blueberries helped keep the ghosts out of your head."

"Was she...?" Lorna let her words linger unsaid. Vivien appeared behind her.

"A little kooky?" Jacob nodded. "Yeah, she was. I

don't think she ever met a superstition she didn't like. She believed in masks on All Hallows Eve to trick demons, and she always put a line of brick dust in the doorways and windows. She was convinced Mrs. Martha across the street was a psychic vampire. The busybody neighbor was tiresome, to be sure. But, when it mattered, my grandma was rarely wrong."

"So, you'd be into a woman who was a little," Vivien tilted her head back and forth as she pretended to search for the right word, "witchy."

"Uh?" Jacob looked to Nina for guidance.

"I think it's obvious that Vivien is trying to ask you out on a date," Nina stated, keeping a straight face. "She won't stop flirting with you."

"What, oh, no, I, wow, no," Vivien stuttered.

Nina laughed. "Just kidding."

Lorna grinned. "She got you."

"Sorry, you left me wide open for that one." Nina picked a blueberry off her muffin. "The cupid-match-maker thing was getting a little weird."

Vivien shrugged. "Can't say it is the first time I've overstepped, probably not the last. I can't help myself. Sometimes I just know things, and they tumble out of my mouth. And, honestly, I'm too old to start changing my ways. I prefer to throw every-thing out and see where it lands.

"Sure, there is a name for that," Jacob said.

"Verbal diarrhea?" Lorna suggested.

"No, it's like clairvoyant, but not clairvoyant." Jacob redirected his attention toward Vivien. "Intuitive."

"Claircognizant," Vivien answered with a nod of approval. "I could tell right away that you were open-minded."

Nina tried not to feel jealous. She had been teasing about the flirting, but Vivien had a natural vivaciousness that would be hard for any man to resist.

"I've got a bit of that instinct myself," Jacob said. "Proves handy as an investigator."

Was *he* flirting with Vivien? Nina thought about excusing herself from the room.

"Right." Vivien sat on the couch across from them. "I can see that. Being able to determine if someone is lying, or guilty, or hiding something. You've spent some time around psychics. I can tell. You've seen some things, haven't you?"

Jacob's tone was guarded. "I can tell there is something strange happening in this house. You ladies are hiding something."

"Is there?" Vivien smiled and leaned back as if accepting a challenge. "What makes you think that?"

"Heather keeps focusing her attention past me like she's seeing an invisible friend whose voice she's actively trying to ignore. It could be a delusion. It could be that she's trying to come up with lies to tell. Lorna is guarded but seems to genuinely care about people. You hide behind bold comments as if hoping to distract from what is really happening."

Okay, so not flirting. He was interrogating.

Vivien's smile didn't falter. "Keep going, Sherlock."

"Jacob," Nina whispered. She didn't want them to get into an argument. She had nowhere else to go.

"No, it's all right," Vivien said. "He's looking out for you. From what I've been sensing, I think you need all the emotional support you can get."

"You're right. I do have feelings for Nina. Strong ones. I've had them since the first night we met, and they've only grown the more I've gotten to know her." Jacob looked at Nina and smiled, completely unashamed of the admission. "I hope someday she'll say the same about me."

Nina tried to think of a response. Nothing came.

She thought she should have been annoyed with Vivien, but instead, she remained calm. There was a feeling of steadiness coming from the woman. Nina trusted her. The realization defied logic, but there it was. Trust. She trusted all of them.

"Everyone has secrets," Vivien said, "but I think you can handle the truth, Jacob. We're magical. I'm psychic, more than you realize. Lorna has the ability to heal and find missing things. She tracked down Nina's car for her. Heather isn't delusional. She sees ghosts. You have one following you. We were discussing whether or not to tell you about it in the kitchen."

Jacob started to turn his head but kept his eyes on Vivien. "She's here now, isn't she?"

Nina looked behind him, unable to see anything standing behind the couch. Was this some kind of joke? Her hand shook as she reached into the empty space, unsure what she thought to find.

Vivien's voice drew her attention back around. "Don't ask me. I can't see ghosts without a spell."

"Can she hear me?" Jacob folded his hands together and gripped them tightly.

"Probably. Sometimes. Depending on the energy she has. If she's following you, she's active. Residual hauntings that are unaware of their surroundings tend to be stuck in a repetitive action. The problem with active hauntings is we can't hear them, and they are stuck trying to get their message across," Vivien said. "You want us to help you with that?"

Jacob didn't readily answer.

"I understand perfectly," Vivien said as if she heard him respond. She stood. "Sure, we'll help you. The sooner you believe us, the sooner you can really be of use in protecting Nina."

"What do you need me to do?" he asked.

And just like that. Jacob was on board. Nina couldn't believe how easily he accepted what was happening. She'd seen things with her own eyes but still had difficulty believing them.

"We need time to prepare. Meet us downtown tonight. Seven o'clock. Warrick Theater." Vivien waved for Nina to follow as she started to leave the room. "Nina, when you're ready, we'll talk in the dining room."

When they were alone, Nina gestured toward Jacob and the spot Vivien had been before encompassing the entire room. "Am I out of touch, or is this just weird?"

"I can't believe I'm saying this, but I think this is where you need to be right now. I have the strongest feeling these women might be able to help you," Jacob said. "Maybe we should rain check lunch."

Nina nodded. "I can't believe I'm agreeing with you, but I think so too."

"But it's only a rain check," he insisted. "Don't change your mind."

"I won't."

Jacob stood. "Look, why don't I swing by the police department and update them on the car? I'll get a copy of the report for your insurance for any damage. I'll bring it by the theater tonight. We can talk more then."

Nina glanced behind him and still didn't see a ghost. "Will you be all right?"

She wanted to ask who he thought was there but refrained. As someone who didn't want people asking questions about her life, she had to respect other people's privacy.

"I've had the feeling of being followed for a long time. A few more hours won't change anything. It's nice to have confirmation." Jacob lightly rubbed his hand along her arm.

"So, you believe in all this? Witches and ghosts and psychics?"

"Don't you? You're here, aren't you? You're staying." He released her arm and cupped his hand against her cheek. "Call me if things get too strange. I'll come right back."

"I will. Thank you." Nina watched him go. Her gaze lingered on his butt before she realized she was staring.

When the door shut, Vivien reappeared. "That boy is *crrrrazy* about you. Normally I only sense that much pining from the High School Geek Club when a tasty cheerleader flips by in her short skirt."

"He's not a geek, and I'm not a cheerleader," Nina corrected.

"My point exactly." Vivien still couldn't seem to help herself as she smiled. "I'll tell you what I told Sue when she was first coming to terms with all this newness. You need to trust yourself more, trust your instincts. There is magic in the world. We can't always see it or express it, but we all look for its connections. We yearn to tell our secrets, even when we know it's risky. We want others to know us. It's the human condition."

Nina wasn't sure where this little speech was going, so she waited.

"Let yourself feel those connections. You can, can't you?" Vivien held up her hand to show her antique ring. "It's humming right there, waiting for you to let it in. I see those connections better than others, but it is in you to find them. I know you must see the way Jacob looks at you. I see the way you look at him. There are these two giant pulsing auras fighting to connect fully."

Nina touched the ring, feeling it vibrate against her.

Vivien waved her hand in dismissal. "But forget falling in love and having explosive sex for a moment."

"My hand feels funny." Nina tried to pull the ring off.

"It won't come off. Not yet. Not while you still need it. After that, you won't want to take it off. They're a gift from Grandma Julia."

They kept talking about this Julia like she was some guru...

Or cult leader.

"Wait, explosive?" Nina asked before she realized what she was saying and to whom she was saying it. "Never mind. Don't answer that."

"Oh, yeah. The vibes are there." Vivien nodded. "Sex at our age is so much better, don't you think? All those body image worries and insecurities just fall away."

Nina arched a brow. "I'm not sure I know the kind of women you're talking about. Most are trying to fight the march of time with a broadsword."

Vivien shrugged. "Well, it *should* be like that for

women our age. When we're young, everything is new and exciting and shiny, but we're not taught how to be assertive. We rarely know what we want or how to ask for it. I really hope that changes for this new generation. They seem to be doing things differently. Say what you like about Gen Z but those zoomers are kicking it up a notch."

Nina looked at her hand. "You were saying about the ring?"

Vivien didn't take the not-so-subtle change of subject as she continued, "Women over forty, we're mature. We know what we want. We know what we're doing. We're not going to put up with fake orgasms or giving in if we don't want sex."

"Again, I'm not sure whom you're talking about. I don't think people turn forty, and a magical fairy just flutters down and makes us secure. It's a nice fairy tale, but I'm less secure now than I used to be."

"Huh." Vivien looked at Nina's hair. "I had thought with your streaks of gray you were embracing the whole next chapter thing."

Nina automatically touched her head.

Vivien's expression fell. "I'm sorry. That struck a nerve. I have some hair color upstairs that would look great on you."

"They said my gray happened as a reaction to

fear." Nina pushed her hair back from her face. "You said the rings can help us. How? I don't want to be terrified of life anymore."

"They amplify what is already there, naturally." Vivien came closer. "Concentrate on me. An invisible force connects all living things. Tap into that force. Try to feel what is coming from me toward you. Know that my intentions are authentic by feeling them for yourself."

As the woman spoke, Nina felt her truth. She nodded slowly.

"And when I focus on you, I feel your pain and fear. It's like your feet are trapped in tar. You're trying to move forward but..." Vivien tilted her head and narrowed her gaze.

"I'm stuck," Nina whispered. "Every time I manage to step in a direction, someone else stops my progress."

"I see that," Vivien agreed. "But you're here now. We're going to unstick your feet. We're going to protect you. Whatever is causing this bad luck of yours, we're going to stop it. Do you believe me?"

Nina nodded. "Yes."

"Good. Now pick up that muffin, and let's eat breakfast. We're going to need all the energy we can get today."

Nina glanced down, realizing she'd set the muffin on the coffee table without meaning to. The anxiety about eating wasn't there. It all came back to trust.

"Do you really think Jacob—?" Nina realized Vivien had already left the room.

She remained on the couch and took a deep breath. There was a lot to take in, and Nina didn't know where to start. Explosive sex. Witches and magic. Jacob had a ghost. She potentially had six ghosts.

That last thought brought her up short, and she quickly stood. She looked around the empty room. A shiver ran over her as she hurried to follow Vivien.

CHAPTER NINE

WARRICK THEATER

Nina crumbled the cookie in her hand, letting the tiny crumbs fall onto the sidewalk as she walked behind the others. The level of sugar these women consumed was remarkable. They insisted it helped with the séance, or recovering from the séance, or something. But after a big breakfast, a giant mid-afternoon dinner, and countless snacks, Nina couldn't force herself to take another bite.

In fact, being as they were all women in their forties, Nina wasn't sure how Lorna, Vivien, and Heather did it. If Nina looked at a picture of a cake, her ass gained weight.

The day had been different from what Nina had expected. Heather had a renter emergency. Someone's boyfriend had tried to rewire a house. The words "wrestling lights" had been used. Then Lorna had to run to work for a few hours. That left her alone with Vivien for most of the day.

Vivien was a master at evading questions and changing the subject. She even convinced Nina to let her cut and color her hair. Finally, Nina had given up trying to pry answers out of her.

Nina watched groups of people come out of the Chinese restaurant across the street. The quaint downtown area fit right in with most small towns in the American South. Everything was considered historic. Markers were affixed to several brick store-fronts to attest to their importance. Though she couldn't see the ocean from where she stood, the smell of the sea drifted through the streets as if carried by the seagulls overhead.

Catching her reflection in the theater's glass door, Nina stared for a moment. Her hair was lighter, and the gray now looked like highlights. A touch of makeup and a hair straightener melted years off her face, mostly because she didn't look tired anymore. Say what you want about embracing your age; there was something to be said about looking your best doing it. She'd almost worn a dress but instead opted for jeans and a long cardigan.

"Another?" Lorna offered a cookie.

"No thanks." Nina shook her head.

Heather leaned against the building and dug in her purse for her keys. They had been a little vague with the exact details of how this would work but insisted it was easier to show than explain. Nina had seen enough television to guess what a séance might look like, but she'd never thought she'd willingly walk into one.

Nina lifted her phone to check the news. She refreshed the screen, expecting the same articles to reappear. Instead, a new one showed. Her chest tightened as she read the title, *"Behind the Mask of a Murderer: Robert Chester Teeter, the Play Doctor Killer."*

Her hands shook, more with rage than anything else. What was it with people's fascination with the depraved? Nina had seen behind that mask. He wasn't sad or misunderstood or had a poor boohoo childhood. He was a fucking monster who did not deserve attention. That's what he wanted. Attention. But it wasn't a mystery. He killed because he liked killing. Period.

Fuck!

"All right, so what happens now?" Nina prompted, turning off the screen. "We're meeting ghost Julia, right? And Julia will be able to tell us how to stop the bad luck?"

"Hopefully," Heather mumbled, still digging in her purse. She had a large messenger bag slung around her chest. It bounced on her hip when she moved, and she pushed it behind her back out of the way.

"I'll call Sue and tell her we're here. She's at the bookstore and will walk down to meet us." Vivien pulled her phone out of her purse and paced a few feet away.

Nina turned on her phone, looked at the article title, and then shut it back off. She took a calming breath. Teeter was still in prison. That's all she needed to know.

"Tell her to bring coffee," Heather called to Vivien. "I need a fix. Marianne's newest boyfriend is into backyard wrestling."

"Is this tap-into-the-sewer-hot-tub-installation guy?" Lorna asked.

"Nope." Heather sighed loudly. "This is a new-new boyfriend. He wears a fake padded muscle shirt and calls himself The Incredible Bulk. I wish she would find a nice stamp collector."

"We start the tour here." Lorna directed her attention at Nina and pointed at a historical marker on the theater's exterior wall. In an overly pleasant tour guide voice, she stated, "Julia Warrick, local businesswoman and suspected witch, commissioned this building in the early nineteen-hundreds. The current city administration likes to dismiss this as a colorful chapter in North Carolina's history because they're fuddy-duddies, but there is no escaping the truth of the past. Julia was a popular medium. As a leader in the spiritualist movement, she held séances in her namesake theater, where she communicated with the dead. Want to know where late Aunt Penny hid the family fortune? Julia could ask her for you. People would travel hundreds of miles to go to one of her sessions. People paid what they could for the service. During the Great Depression, some of her clients paid with food items, like chickens and potatoes."

"Tell her about the pot farm," Vivien said before returning to her phone conversation.

"What this plaque doesn't say, and what the city will never acknowledge, is that Julia Warrick bought several properties in town and constructed this building with money she made bootlegging moonshine and growing marijuana during Prohibition."

"That's my gangster grandma," Heather muttered.

"She was also a Burlesque dancer, played piano in a jazz club, wrote a recipe column for the paper, and owned a hotel that mysteriously burned down in the 1950s." Lorna moved to where Heather finally managed to unlock one of the doors. It was the only way inside, as it stood next to a long row of glass doors with security locks. The long metal handles across the front interiors of each security door would allow people to leave but not reenter.

Nina leaned close to the glass. The windows did little to hide the dark art deco interior. There was enough light shining through to show two restroom signs along one side, and a concession stand near the back.

"Julia's granddaughter, Heather Harrison, now owns the building. Today the old theater pulls in an entirely different kind of clientele. Managed by yours truly," Lorna framed her hands around her face, "we officially host indie film screenings, retro movie nights, ballet recitals, orchestra concerts, award ceremonies, and even an Elvis impersonator."

"Are you done?" Heather asked, holding the door.

"Almost. Hold on," Lorna answered before lowering her voice to sound mysterious. "But, on some nights, like tonight, we are closed to the public and get together to celebrate all that Julia has taught us."

"Now are you done?" Heather prompted.

"Yeah. Open it." Lorna's voice returned to normal.

"That was very dramatic. You've been working with the theater kids too long," Heather teased.

"It was theater camp last week," Lorna explained as she held open the door for Nina. "I gave a lot of ghost Julia tours. Of course, none of them left here with actual evidence. I'm working on putting together a Halloween haunted theater tour. Haunted reputations are very big these days. I'm trying to convince Heather we need to play it up and sell merchandise."

Nina cautiously followed the women inside.

"Julia would love the notoriety," Lorna insisted.

"I'm sure she would." Heather moved directly to the light switches, flipping a few of them on. The concession stand lit up, but the front lobby lights stayed low. Thick red curtains hung on either side.

"Candy?" Lorna asked Nina.

"No, thanks. I'm good." Nina shook her head.

"Offer is open. Feel free to grab sodas or snacks anytime you want," Lorna said.

The theater was clean and well cared for but

severely out-of-date. Burgundy and gold sponge paint covered the walls to accent the art deco molding. There was an energy in the air, a charge so electric she felt it crawling over her body. The vibrations from the ring became almost painful. She shook her hand, trying to get them to stop.

Vivien paced across the front windows, still on the phone. A man in a suit strode past her as if he had better places to be.

Nina looked around the lobby. It was in full view of the street. "Where do we do this?"

"Theater stage." Lorna gestured toward the curtains by the concessions.

A tiny chill worked over her, and she stared into a dark area past the restrooms. She wasn't sure if it was her imagination or if something was really there watching them.

"It's just my office and a storeroom over there," Lorna said.

Nina looked in the other direction.

"Down that hall is alley access. But be careful. The door locks behind you if you go out that way," Lorna continued.

Nina again felt a chill like she was being watched and turned to stare toward Lorna's office. She studied the shadows, trying to detect movement.

"You're safe here," Heather said, her voice soft. Out of all the friends, she presented as the most emotionally guarded.

Nina realized, despite the feeling of being watched, she felt safe in the building. The knot of fear had eased its hold over her chest. But it wasn't just the building. It was knowing the others were there with her. It had been so long since she'd felt anything close to this. She became afraid to move as if that might shatter the illusion and she'd stop being able to breathe.

"Hey." Heather touched her arm. The contact sent tiny jolts of emotions through Nina. She detected Heather's concern. "Lean into this. I've seen ghosts my whole life. Almost all are harmless. They're just lost people lingering where we can't see them, where they can't touch us. Tonight, we're going to do a séance so that the rest of you can see them as well, briefly, only during the ritual. Then we're going to send them away again."

Vivien came inside. "Sue's on her way." She lifted her hands toward Lorna at the concessions. "Chocolate me!"

Lorna threw a candy bar at Vivien.

A door rattled. Nina glanced toward the

windows. The man in the suit stood glaring in as he searched the theater lobby.

"Who's that?" Lorna asked.

"No clue," Vivien answered.

The man's eyes found Nina, and he smiled. The cruel expression did not feel welcoming as his eyes narrowed. He lifted a finger and tapped it against the glass in her direction as if trying to poke her.

"Nina?" Heather asked.

"I don't know him," she whispered, shaking her head.

"Heather, is there a ghost influencing him?" Vivien dropped the candy and joined them.

"I don't see anything." Heather stepped in front of Nina to block her from the man's view.

Vivien strode toward the door and yelled, "What do you want, creep? She's not interested."

The man pushed at the door, rattling it but unable to get inside. He kept trying to stare at Nina.

"Sue's coming," Lorna warned as she rushed past. "We have to stop her."

Sue walked toward the man.

"Back off!" Vivien yelled, forcing his attention to turn toward her. She ran through the unlocked door and stepped onto the sidewalk.

Sue came to a surprised stop.

Seeing the open door, the man began to stride toward it, repeatedly glancing at Nina as he moved.

Vivien didn't hesitate. She drew back her arm and thrust the heel of her hand upward into the man's jaw. His head snapped back, and he stumbled with a loud groan.

"What the hell is your problem, lady?" he yelled, holding his face. He glanced around in confusion before taking off across the street toward the Chinese restaurant.

Sue approached cautiously. "What was that?"

"Dude was creeping on Nina," Vivien said before shouting, "Yeah, you better run. Don't let me see you around here again!"

"Crazy bitch," he yelled.

"Asshole!" Vivien flipped him off and then pushed the door to hold it open for Sue. As if nothing had happened, she reached for a coffee. "Oh, yum, thank you."

Vivien took a sip while shaking out her punching hand.

"Does that happen to you a lot?" Lorna asked Nina.

"Usually not that aggressive," she said. "At least not directly toward me. The last guy who looked at me like that stole my car."

"Well, I didn't try to fix it yet, so no worries there. That jerk isn't taking your car anywhere," Sue said as she passed out coffees. "I had Jameson add extra shots of espresso." She paused to smile at Nina. "It's good to see you again. I'm glad you decided to come tonight."

Nina nodded her thanks.

"That guy's lucky Viv aimed for his face and not his balls," Heather said.

"Thought about it," Vivien quipped, latching the door. "Oh, man, I wish someone was recording that. Troy is going to be so proud he insisted we take that self-defense class."

"Troy?" Nina asked Lorna.

"Her manfriend," Lorna explained.

"So tonight? Vivien said something on the phone about Nina's boyfriend. We're helping him talk to a spirit?" Sue asked.

"He's not—" Nina started to protest.

"Here yet," Vivien finished for her. "Ladies, should we start?"

Heather pulled the strap of her messenger bag over her head. "Let's do this. I have new candles and oils."

Heather walked through the curtains to the right of the concessions. The others followed.

Nina glanced toward the sidewalk. Seeing a family walk past, she ducked behind the curtains as their father looked in and saw her. She didn't need a stranger glaring and coming after her in front of his children. There was no telling what would set people off.

Amphitheater seats lined up before a black stage. A movie screen was partially lowered behind it. Aisles led from the curtains to the front. It wasn't a huge theater, and the décor looked as antiquated as the rest of the building.

Heather made her way onto the stage. She dropped her messenger bag on the floor. "Grandma? Are you here?"

Was this it? Nina stopped halfway down and searched the seats.

Heather flipped on the stage lights. "We'll have a couple of guests tonight that I'd like you to say hi to."

Nina again looked around and only saw the other women.

"Hi, Jules," Vivien said, raising her voice, so it carried over the amphitheater.

Nina didn't hear an answer.

"Hey, Julia," Lorna added.

"Hi, Julia," Sue said. "Can't wait to see you again."

Nina looked and listened. Still nothing.

"She says," Heather grimaced, "something highly inappropriate."

"That's my girl," Vivien laughed. She held up her phone. "Come check it out. I have new videos for you to watch."

"Viv," Heather scolded.

"What?" Vivien lowered the phone and grumbled, "I'll show you later, Julia."

"Grandma, listen," Heather said, looking down from the stage at an empty chair. "Fine, *Julia*. Julia, listen, we have another ring bearer who needs our help. Also—"

Heather looked slightly annoyed as she took a deep breath as if someone had cut off her words.

"Also, we have a customer." Heather nodded. "Yes, that's right. He has a spirit attached to him and we're going to help them communicate." Heather shook her head. "No, I don't know what he's willing to pay for it." She again nodded. "Right, right, I'll be sure not to charge too much." And then shook her head once more. "I know, I know, no charity. People have pride and will want to give something. I promise I won't humiliate him by refusing payment, but he's a friend, so we're not asking for anything."

"This must be younger Julia she's talking to,"

Lorna said, approaching Nina. "It'd be the version of Julia before she became a mother or grandmother."

"Martin is well, thank you, and no, I'm not going to discuss my sex life with you," Heather said. "Just, please, behave tonight. We have a lot of work ahead of us."

"I'll tell you all about my sex life," Vivien offered the ghost as she made her way onto the stage.

"Stop encouraging her," Heather scolded.

Vivien laughed. "You say encourage. I say entertain."

Nina leaned closer to Lorna. "Where is she?"

"I'm guessing wherever Heather is looking," Lorna answered. "Don't worry. Nothing has changed, only you're more aware that someone might be where you can't see them. It's like walking past cold air at most. She won't hurt you."

Nina glanced at Heather to find her looking directly at her. A chill worked over her, and she inadvertently took several steps forward before turning around.

As if the world wasn't bad enough. Now she had to look out for invisible threats. With each passing second, the path she was on became more real.

Not that Julia was a threat.

But that didn't mean other ghosts weren't causing her problems.

"She's gone for now," Heather said, drawing Nina's attention back to the stage. She pulled a large item wrapped in a blue cloth out of her messenger bag and laid it on the stage floor.

"You should check this out," Lorna said. "It's the book I was telling you about that I found under the stage."

"The grimoire?" Nina clarified.

Lorna nodded.

Nina followed her up the small flight of stairs onto the stage. Vivien unwrapped the book on the floor as Heather pulled blue candles out of her bag.

Nina stood over Vivien to watch. The padded leather cover looked old and handcrafted, which was not surprising considering what it was. Symbols were embossed in a circular pattern on the top. Nina saw the oval shape of her ring amongst them. Her finger tingled.

Nina glanced at Vivien's hand as she smoothed down the cloth. Her ring also matched a symbol on the book. The same pattern had been sewn onto the fabric.

Heather placed four candles around the edges of

the material before anointing them with oil. The smell of basil settled heavily in the air.

"What are you doing?" Nina asked.

"The blue helps amplify our messages to the dead for the séance," Lorna explained, coming to stand beside her. "The oil provides protection from ill-tempered spirits."

Nina watched as Vivien fussed with smoothing wrinkles out of the cloth.

Lorna pulled a candy bar out of her pocket. "Sugar because you're going to feel exhausted after we're done. Normally I'll make cupcakes or scones, but I didn't have time to get to the grocery store today."

"Speaking of groceries..." Heather glanced at Lorna.

"Yeah, William and I took care of it yesterday. Mr. Willis is all set. I told him, no more pizza." Lorna gave a small laugh. "I found two empty boxes hidden in his closet, though. I think he just likes the attention. William is taking him fishing next week."

Nina glanced around the group.

"Mr. Willis is a retired tenant of Heather's," Sue explained. "He doesn't have family, so we all try to check in on him. If we leave him alone too long, he'll live on nothing but pizza deliveries."

Nina nodded, not really wanting to digress into tenants and pizza, considering what they were at the theater to do. She kneeled on the floor and gestured to the book. "May I?"

"Go ahead," Vivien said.

Nina reached for the book. She sat down on the hard floor and placed it on her lap as she opened the cover. The old pages felt as if they had a life of their own when she touched them. The title page read, "*Warrick.*" All the entries were handwritten in a beautiful calligraphy. There were lists of names and dates.

Sue kneeled next to her. "Those are the people Julia helped, what they paid, etcetera." She pointed at an entry and read, "*December 12, 1930, Walt Walters, two cents to contact wife. Lost love. Heartbreaking. Mary refuses to move on without him.*"

Heather glanced over her shoulder. "Julia says she remembers the man. He killed himself a week later to be with her."

Julia had apparently returned. Nina looked for the ghost.

"Beautiful and tragic," Sue whispered as she flipped deeper into the book. Touching the page, she said, "These are suggested séance-y things."

"Séance-y things?" Lorna laughed.

Nina started to read, "*Spirits tethered—*"

"Whoa, no!" Vivien gasped.

Sue put her hand over the words to stop Nina.

"Not yet," Heather added.

"Not out loud," Sue said. "Silent reading only."

Nina glanced around the theater, not finding anything before turning back to read, "*Spirits tethered to this plane we humbly seek your guidance. Spirits search amongst your numbers for a lost child, we call forth...*" A blank space was left between the words. "*...from the great beyond.*"

And then the next section.

"*We open the door between two worlds to call forth the spirit of...*" Another blank spot. "*Come back from the grave so that we may hear. Come back from the grave and show yourself to us so that all may see. Come back from the grave and answer for what you have done so that you may be judged.*"

And still the next.

"*Beings tethered to this plane, full of rage and filled with pain. We call you to come near. We call you to face what you fear. We call you to your eternal hell. Pay the price with this final knell.*"

Nina pointed at the word rage. "Can they...?"

"We won't use that one," Sue assured her.

"No demon fighting tonight," Vivien muttered.

"Demons?" Nina closed the book and handed it to Sue. No one said anything about demons. She didn't sign on for that.

"She's just..." Heather waved her hand in dismissal. "Don't worry about all that."

It wasn't much of a reassurance.

They fell into silence. Nina focused her attention on their surroundings, listening for signs that something might be more than the creak of an old building or the electric buzz of overhead lights.

A loud ding sounded, and she yelped in surprise. It took a moment to realize it was her cell phone. She scrambled to her feet and pulled it from her pocket. "It's Jacob texting. He's outside."

"Look at that. Right on time." Vivien stood as Sue returned the book to the blue cloth. "I'll go let him in."

CHAPTER TEN

"This is one hell of a first date," Jacob whispered as he reached to take Nina's hand. "Thank you for doing this for me."

For the briefest of moments, she forgot what they were undertaking as she looked into his eyes. She couldn't fathom what he saw in her. She was a mess —untrusting, fearful, and stressed all the time. Yet, here he was, bluntly stating yet again what his intentions were.

"*Uh-hem,*" Vivien cleared her throat.

"Do you know her name?" Heather looked expectantly at Jacob. "She's focused on you and doesn't seem to see me, so I can't talk to her like this. She has short black hair, brown eyes, and a scar over her collarbone. Looks young, but that doesn't always mean they died young."

Jacob nodded. "Ester, my mother. I started feeling her after she died when I was a boy. I used to think I could see her when I was a teenager. It'd be like a glimpse in the mirror when I was drunk, so it was always dismissed as a trick of the mind."

"How young were you?" Nina asked.

"Not old enough to be drunk," he admitted. "Truth be told, I developed a little problem for a while in hopes that I could see her. It finally occurred to me that is not what she would have wanted."

"I mean, how young when you lost her," Nina clarified.

"Oh. Ten," he answered.

"I'm sorry." Nina squeezed his hand. "That couldn't have been easy."

Nina realized she had been selfish in their friendship. She had been so wrapped up in what had happened to her that she hadn't asked him more about himself. She made a self-promise to do better in her relationships with others.

"You ready to see some magic?" Vivien asked, taking Jacob's other hand. "Everyone form a circle and keep off the séance cloth."

Heather stood between Lorna and Sue. Lorna

gave Nina's hand a small squeeze. They formed a joined circle around the cloth and book.

Heather looked around to make sure they were ready before stating, "It is our intention to talk to Jacob's mother, Ester."

Small flames erupted over the candle wicks as they lit themselves.

Nina gasped. Jacob drew closer to her, not releasing her hand.

Energy flowed through her as if swimming around them from hand to hand. She searched the circle, trying to decipher what she felt. The emotions were distinct, like a signature or a person's voice.

Lorna genuinely wanted to help everyone feel better. She would put everyone else's feelings and needs before her own. The mothering instinct inside of her was strong.

Heather seemed determined. Though she seemed at peace, a deep sadness had left its scars. Those scars had created a wall that made her guarded around others. She'd lost someone close to her. For some reason, and without any proof, Nina thought it might be a child.

Sue was nervous with anticipation like she was about to climb onto a dangerous roller coaster.

Vivien was having fun. The woman enthusiastically charged into whatever task was put in front of her. One word filtered through Nina's mind as she looked at the woman. Fearless. Vivien was fearless. The others seemed to envy that quality in her.

And then there was Jacob...

Nina felt him as if his spirit moved inside of her. He desperately wanted to protect her. That need warred with a strong desire to be around her. He had not lied. He wanted her like a man wanted a woman. He tried to suppress that desire to act like a gentleman, but the fantasies in his head had nothing to do with gentlemanly pursuits.

Feeling amusement, Nina turned her attention to Vivien. The woman grinned at her and nodded as if to say, "Told you so."

What had Vivien said to her at the house?

"All living things are connected by an invisible force. Tap into that force."

Nina got what that meant now.

With all her new insights, she worried about what the others might sense about her. Of course, there would be her fear. That was always there, but would they see what happened? Would they know all the things she couldn't form into words? The guilt she felt in surviving, knowing what the others had gone through, even though it had happened before she'd been brought to the doctor's playroom?

They were all looking at her like they saw the truth. Her hands began to shake, and she started to pull away. She waited for their pity.

"Don't let go," Heather instructed. "Not until we do first."

Nina nodded that she understood. Jacob held her tighter. Their pity never came.

The magical energy between them built with a confused mingling of emotions until it felt as if they were one being in six separate bodies. The tingling in her hands worked its way over her body, and her hair began to lift from her shoulders. She shivered as gooseflesh erupted on her skin. The others experienced the same thing as their hair floated around them. It was as if they were all the result of a static electricity science experiment.

"It's ok, Nina," Jacob whispered. "I won't leave your side."

"I know." She tried to smile in reassurance.

The stage lights flickered. Nina looked at the ceiling.

"Ghosts need energy to manifest," Lorna explained. "That's supposed to happen. Don't be surprised if they drain our cell phones too."

Vivien, Heather, Sue, and Lorna began speaking in unison. "Spirits tethered to this plane we humbly seek your guidance. Spirits search amongst your numbers for a lost mother, we call forth Ester from the great beyond."

Twinkling lights formed over the book. The ring on Nina's finger pulsed. The lights began to move, dancing like a tornado of lightning bugs as they created a small funnel. Nina couldn't look away, couldn't even bring herself to blink.

"Spirits tethered to this plane we humbly seek your guidance," the women repeated. "Spirits search amongst your numbers for a lost mother, we call forth Ester from the great beyond."

Transparent dress shoes appeared over the book, hovering in the air. As the lights rose higher, legs appeared to grow from the shoes—first calves and then knees.

"Mom?" Jacob whispered in awe.

A skirt formed into a dress. There appeared to be tiny dots of flowers in the fabric. Nina saw Heather through the ghost's body. The candlelight seemed to reflect from within the spirit to give her shape. Finally, Ester's head appeared. Black hair had been cut in the wedge style popular in the seventies. The short, angular locks framed a sad face. Large glasses encased milky eyes. She gazed at her son.

Heather released Sue and Lorna. She stepped back and slowly walked around the circle to the other side. Lorna let go of Nina.

Jacob held on tighter. "Can I...?"

Vivien had let him go, and he reached forward. Ester's head tilted.

"She looks tired." Jacob didn't make contact. "And so sad."

"She's been lingering for a long time." Heather put her hand on his shoulder. "Go ahead. Talk to her."

"Hi," Jacob whispered before clearing his throat. "Hi, Mom."

The spirit blinked.

"It's good to finally see you again," he said. "I've missed you."

Ester's brow furrowed.

"It's Jacob."

"Jacob?" The ghost blinked again as if coming awake. She smiled as she looked him over. "You're so big."

"You look just as I remember you." He didn't release Nina's hand, but his fingers tightened and loosened nervously.

"How can you be so big?" Ester hands stirred at her sides, but she didn't move from her place hovering over the book.

Nina glanced at Jacob but couldn't keep from staring at Ester for too long. Even as she saw the evidence of an afterlife with her own eyes, this felt surreal.

"It's been nearly forty years since you died," he said.

Ester lifted her hands and stared at them. "No. I'm waiting for something. I can't go."

"What are you waiting for?"

"Jacob?" Ester smiled at her son. "You're so big. How can you be so big?"

"I told you. It's been nearly forty years."

"No. That's not right." Ester shook her head. "I'm waiting for something. Are you waiting?"

"Mom?"

"Jacob? Is that you?" Ester again smiled at him. "You're so big. How can you be so big?"

"Mom?" Jacob frowned. He turned to the others. "What's wrong with her?"

"She's looping," Vivien said.

"She's been drifting for a long time," Heather answered. "Tell her a memory you have of her. A good one. Connect her to her past, to who she once was."

Jacob nodded. "Mom, do you remember when I was six years old, and we were supposed to go to the beach? On the way there a semi-truck overturned in the road."

"I said something good," Heather interrupted.

"We had to take a detour and ended up at an indoor ice rink in our swimsuits. You told me, water is water, we were just swimming on top of it. Afterward, we had a picnic in the hotel parking lot. You said it was the best day at the beach you'd ever had. When I went back to school, I told the teacher I'd walked on water for summer vacation, but she didn't believe me."

"You had the rosiest little cheeks." Ester smiled. The overhead lights flickered and for a moment it appeared as if Ester would fade.

"Ask her what she needs to tell you," Heather prompted.

Jacob stepped closer. "Mom, what are you waiting for? Do you need me to know something?"

"Yes. There is something. Something important I need to tell you." Ester nodded.

"What?" Jacob's foot landed on the cloth. Nina released his hand.

Ester stepped down off the book and came toward him. She looked up at him and tried to touch his cheek. Her fingers swept into his face. Jacob put his hand on his cheek where hers had disappeared.

"Listen carefully," Ester said, leaning closer. "Your blankie is in the blue box in the hallway closet. Your father hid it there, but I know my big boy sleeps better with it."

"Uh...?" Jacob tilted his head to the side.

Vivien suppressed a laugh.

"What?" Sue mouthed before covering her lips.

"My blankie?" Jacob repeated.

Ester nodded. "I've been so worried you wouldn't find it."

"Okay. I'll look," he promised.

Ester's shoulders lifted and fell as if she let loose a long sigh of relief. "Sweet boy, I didn't want to leave you."

"You didn't leave me. You've always been with me. You'll always be with me." Jacob touched his chest. "Here."

Ester looked at Nina and smiled. "Introduce me."

"Oh, uh, Nina," Jacob turned slightly to look at her.

"Nina," Ester repeated.

Nina had no idea what she should say to a ghost.

"Do you love him?" Ester asked.

"Mom, it's still new," Jacob answered for her.

"Don't waste time. There is so very little of it." Ester flickered as the overhead lights tried to come back on.

"Jacob, we need to help her move on," Heather said.

Jacob shook his head. "I don't think I can. I don't want her to go."

"Don't strand her here," Heather insisted. "Trust me. She's drifted for forty years waiting to give you that message. It's time for her to move on."

"Mom, I love you," Jacob said. "Thank you for everything."

"Jacob?" Ester faded a little more.

"It was nice to meet you, Ester," Nina finally managed to say.

Ester glanced at her and then back at her son. "Jacob? Is that you? How can you be so big?"

"She did what she needed to do," Heather said. "Don't make her earthbound. With her message passed on, she'll not have any purpose."

"Okay." Jacob nodded. "Whatever is best for her."

"You're so big." She touched his face with two hands. "How can you be so big?"

"Spirit you have been found pure," Heather said. "We release you into the light. Go in peace and love."

"How can you be so...?" The light inside Ester's form floated upward like dying embers dancing over a fire before disappearing. The candles extinguished, and the overhead lights turned back on.

They stood in silence for a long moment. Jacob stared up to where his mother had disappeared.

"Jacob?" Nina asked.

His head dropped forward, and his shoulders started to shake.

Nina placed her hand on his back. "I'm so sorry."

Jacob lifted his head and turned to them. He shook harder as he laughed. "Did she say my blankie? She waited around forty years to tell me where to find my blankie."

His laughter prompted the other women to join him.

Nina pressed her lips together. Laughing didn't seem right.

"Oh, we shouldn't laugh," Lorna said, even as she chuckled. "I think it's sweet. She was a mom worried about her baby boy."

"Did you ever find your blankie?" Vivien asked.

"Yes. In high school." Jacob wiped his eyes. "I'm sad to say it had lost its protective powers by then. I think I cut it up to make patches for my jeans."

"I agree," Nina said. "It was very sweet of her. You can tell she loved you very much."

Jacob took a deep breath as he looked around the theater. "I'm a little sad not to feel her presence."

"She's not gone," Lorna said. "Her spirit moved on, but she's your mom. She'll always be with you."

"Thank you," Jacob looked around at each of them. "Thank you for helping her."

"Of course, it's what we do." Vivien smiled. "And now, your turn Miss Nina."

"Oh, wait!" Lorna pulled the candy bar from her pocket. She opened it and broke the candy in half. She gave the pieces to Nina and Jacob. "Sugar first."

Nina ate the candy bar even though she wasn't hungry.

A thud sounded as the cover of the book flew open. Nina took hold of Jacob's arm, and they both backed away. The pages flapped before settling to leave the book open.

They all went forward to watch as the sound of a pen scratched at the parchment. Words appeared as an entry was added to the book. In the same cursive handwriting as the other entries, the date was added to the page, followed by the words, *"Jacob Paddock, a family friend who does not need to pay to contact his mother to put her at peace, Ester Paddock. Successful."*

"Thanks, Julia," Heather said.

"Bye, Mom," Jacob whispered, wiping at his eyes. "Thank you for everything. I love you."

CHAPTER ELEVEN

JACOB STOOD IN SILENCE, staring at the floor where his mother had been. Nina didn't know what to say, so she left him alone. Grief wasn't a straight line, and there was nothing she could think to say that would help him. How did someone say goodbye forty years after the fact?

The hum of the others' emotions lingered inside of her, softer than before but there. She felt as if her life had shifted once again, and she knew nothing would ever be the same. That had happened once before as she lay on a cold metal table. All the truths of her life had been wiped out in one second of awareness.

That had happened again. She'd stepped out of the reality she had known her whole life and now stood on the other side. The paranormal was real. Ghosts were real. There was something after death, an awareness that carried over from life.

Ghosts existed. The dead lingered when they had unfinished business. What did she do with that evidence?

What would her afterlife be? Would she be locked in a moment like a residual? Would she be aware like Ester, desperate to be heard?

Nina couldn't help but fear she would be trapped back on that metal table for all eternity.

She forced her thoughts back to the moment. The afterlife would have to wait. She was alive now and had to deal with the problems in front of her.

Somehow, Nina doubted that whoever was terrorizing her would want to tell her where her childhood security blanket was hidden.

"I'm not going to lie to you," Vivien said, taking a seat next to her in the front row.

Nina turned her attention away from Jacob.

Vivien picked candy pieces out of a box and tossed them into her mouth. "That séance was child's play."

Vivien offered her candy, and Nina shook her head in denial. She was too nervous to eat anything.

"Don't get me wrong, it was sweet to see mother

and son have a moment," she continued, "but I'm guessing it's not your mom possessing people to mess with you."

"She would never," Nina agreed.

"You said earlier that you thought *they* might be haunting you?" Vivien prompted. "Now would be the time to share with us who they are."

"Teeter's other victims," Nina answered. "They're the only ones who died around me. Maybe they're mad at me for living. Or for not helping them in time? I don't know. Do you really think someone is possessing people to terrorize me?"

"It's our best guess. Heather hasn't seen any ghosts hanging around you, but something is causing your bad luck." Vivien set the candy box into the drink holder on the chair. "Were you there when Teeter...?"

Nina shook her head. "Only the last one. He liked to overlap his toys. He wanted us to know what was coming. He wanted us to know there was no way out."

Faint sounds echoed from a hellish place within her memory. She tried to keep that thought-demon locked up tight, but sometimes it spilled out and demanded attention.

"Thought-demon?" Vivien frowned. "You never said anything about a demon."

"Are you in my head?" Nina stood, not liking the idea of her thoughts being read. She pushed her hands against her temples to physically block the intrusion.

"Psychic," Vivien reminded her, patting her hand over her chest. "I pick up fragments."

"Thought-demons. Bad thoughts. It's just something my mother used to call it when people dwelled on the bad things that happened to them and couldn't move on." Nina dropped her hands to her sides. "This is the second time tonight demons have been mentioned. Is that a real concern?"

Vivien didn't readily answer.

"I thought you said you weren't going to lie to me," Nina stated.

Vivien sighed in resignation like a kid caught sneaking candy before dinner. She picked up the box and plucked another piece from inside before dropping it back in. "Yeah, demons are real."

Nina waited for her to expand on that. When Vivien simply stared into the box, shaking it as if trying to find a flavor she wanted, Nina insisted, "And?"

"Oh," Vivien glanced up. "Sorry. I was just

thinking. No, there shouldn't be any demon stuff happening tonight. I mean, the one time we summoned something that bad it was by accident. We were new, and we didn't close the veil between the realms like we were supposed to, and something slipped through. We sent it back. It's all good now. We've gotten much better at séances."

All good now?

Nina simply stood, staring down at Vivien and her candy.

"Are you sure you don't want one?" Vivien asked, offering the box.

"Yeah," Nina answered in disbelief. "I'm positive."

"Anyway." Vivien again set the box down. "First, we'll call Julia. She's got more experience than all of us combined. Then we'll call the six women and try to give them peace. Whether they're behind your bad luck or not, we should help them find peace. No one deserves to linger with that."

Lorna and Sue came from behind the back curtains, carrying their coffees. They walked down the far aisle toward the stage.

Nina nodded. "I'll do anything to help them. After what those women went through... Anything."

Vivien stood and placed her hands on Nina's

shoulders. "Jacob being here is good. Usually, I'm all you don't need a man—*and you don't my amazing woman friend*—but you're better when he's near, calmer. And you have us now. If those thought-demons start to overwhelm you, I want you to look at me. Use our connection. Feel that you're with friends. Feel me telling you that everything is going to be okay."

"I will." Nina took a deep, steadying breath.

"Julia's ready," Heather called down to them. "Let's get her before she manifests as a burlesque dancer."

"What does that mean?" Nina asked.

Vivien led the way out of the row to the stage. "Julia manifests from different eras on her timeline. Sometimes it's Grandma Julia who made cookies and has a handle on her magic, and sometimes it's bootlegger Julia bored and looking to stir a little trouble. And sometimes it's burlesque Julia possessing one of us," Vivien pointed at herself, "and trying to put on a show."

"Do possessions happen a lot?" Nina couldn't imagine something slipping inside of her and taking over.

"What's a lot?" Vivien shrugged, not giving a real answer. "Don't worry. Your ring will protect you.

Julia's the exception since it's rooted in her magic, and I don't think she'd ever do that to you. I've known her my whole life, and she knew I'd have fun."

"Ready?" Heather moved to the edge of the stage.

Nina nodded. Jacob watched her as she walked toward him. He offered his hand as she neared, and she took it. He pulled her close so that only a sliver of air separated them.

"Are you nervous?" he asked.

Nina nodded.

He leaned his head close to hers. "I'm right here. I'm not going anywhere. Whatever happens. I'm in this with you, Nina."

"I know." Nina couldn't stop herself from gravitating into him. "Are *you* okay? I can't imagine what you're feeling right now."

"I will be." Jacob wrapped his arms around her. She felt his hands massaging up and down her back. "I'll miss her presence, but I'm happy she's found peace."

"If you want to talk about it, I'm here. This friendship goes both ways."

"I know it does." He nodded. "Thank you."

"Join hands," Heather said. "We're starting to lose Julia's attention."

Jacob held her for a few more seconds before letting go. He took her hand in his.

"Did you get ahold of the guys and let them know we're all right?" Lorna asked Heather.

"Yeah, they're all at William's watching sports bloopers and eating deep-dish pizza," Heather answered. "There was shouting in the background. It's boy paradise."

"So, what you're saying is I'm going to have to heal a sprayed something later when they're done reenacting whatever it is they are doing?" Lorna nodded. "Got it."

"Exactly," Heather said.

"We intend to talk to Julia Warrick," Vivien announced as they resumed their circle around the séance cloth. The candle wicks erupted into flames.

The zap of energy and emotion rushed over Nina as it came through their joined hands. Their hair lifted off their shoulders. Her heartbeat sped in anticipation and uncertainty. She felt safe with the others around her, but there was no denying what they were doing was dangerous.

"Teeter is in jail," Vivien said, prompting Nina to meet her gaze. "He can't hurt you here. He can't hurt any of them. Stay strong. We're going to get through this."

Nina nodded that she understood. She felt Vivien trying to send her reassurance through their connection.

"He'll get what's coming to him," Heather said.

"We'll make sure of it," Sue added.

"You're not alone," Lorna soothed.

How had this happened? How had she met these wonderful people? Part of her felt as if she didn't deserve it.

A tear slid over her cheek. How could she ever repay this kindness? There was no judgment, no hesitation, only support and love. This was how female friendships were supposed to be.

"Let's do it," Heather said.

"Say the words the best you can," Vivien told Nina.

"Spirits tethered to this plane we humbly seek your guidance," the other women said in unison. Nina joined them, using their words to prompt hers a millisecond behind. "Spirits search amongst your numbers for the spirit we seek. We call forth Julia Warrick from the great beyond."

Nina glanced around as they fell silent. She

turned her attention to the book to watch for Julia to appear.

"What kind of living hell have you brought me?" a woman exclaimed from behind Nina.

Nina gasped and spun around to find a transparent young woman standing close to her. She dropped the hands next to her, forgetting that she was supposed to be part of a circle.

The ghost wore a button-down shirt fastened all the way up to the throat. Her wavy bob and red lipstick belonged at the turn of the 20th century. She had high-waisted trousers and heeled boots with narrow laces running up the front.

"Looks like we didn't get Grandma," Lorna said.

"Julia?" Nina whispered.

The ghost waved her hands in front of Nina's face. "I can't even see her under all this dark smoke. Does she have a face? Is it unfortunate?"

"What smoke?" Heather asked.

"Her aura. It's..." Julia coughed and took several steps back. The softest echoing thud followed the sound of each of her steps.

Nina looked down, trying to see what Julia was seeing. "I don't understand."

"Is she talking?" Julia asked. "It sounds all muffled. What's wrong with her? I mean, I heard about putting a potato sack over someone's head, but this is beyond the—"

"Julia, this is Nina. She found one of your rings," Lorna put forth to stop the insults. "She's a friend, a very beautiful friend."

Julia flicked her hand to the side. A cigarette appeared at the end of a long holder as she brought her hands to her mouth. She inhaled and the look of smoke swirled within her transparent chest. "I can barely breathe next to her. She sucks the air from the room. Maybe she should wait outside."

"Be nice," Heather scolded. "She needs our help."

"Who's that wolf hiding behind the smoke cloud?" Julia gestured her cigarette. "Step out where I can see you, handsome."

Jacob stood next to Nina and should have been in full view of the spirit. He stepped forward. "Hello, ma'am."

"Ma'am is my mother's name," Julia flirted. "Call me your baby doll, and I'll take you to the best juice joint in town. What do you say? Want to blow this chicken coop and find a real party?"

The spirit winked at him.

Jacob moved closer to Nina.

"Oh." Julia frowned. "You're with the storm

cloud. Too bad. Let me know if you change your mind and want a little sunshine. I may be dead, but I'm not *dead,* if you know what I mean."

"Easy," Heather said. "He's taken. We're here for Nina, not your libido. You enchanted the rings to bring us together so that we could help each other heal from our individual pains. Nina is here to heal. Help her. Help us help her."

Julia's spirit was much more aware than Ester had been. If not for her translucence, she acted just as she would have when she was alive. There was no looping or confusion. Her voice was strong and clear, and her gaze sharp. "I don't see a ring. I can't even see a face. How do I know what's hiding under that mess?"

"Why can't she see me?" Nina asked.

"What's she saying?" Julia inquired. "All I hear is *mumf-mumf-mumf-mumf.*"

"She wants to know why you don't see her," Sue said.

"What ring does she have?" Julia's cigarette disappeared and she shoved her hands into her front pockets as she came close to Nina. She leaned over, searching for a hand she couldn't see. Nina felt a chill radiating from the woman.

"Large oval." Lorna held her hands in the shape and size of Nina's ring.

"Oh." Julia instantly straightened. Her expression appeared stunned. "That's bad. I was hoping no one would ever need that one."

"What is it?" Nina asked.

"What is it?" Vivien repeated for her.

Julia faded, stopping short of disappearing altogether. Her face changed as her image reemerged older than before. Lines framed her eyes and mouth. Her trousers flared as they morphed into a skirt, and the button-down became a silky blouse with large flower patterns on it.

"Big ring for big magic for mountain-sized problems." Julia's voice sounded more mature, and her expression was less mischievous.

"Hi, Grandma," Heather said. "Thank you for coming."

"Hi, Pumpkins," Julia answered. "Fill me in. What's happening with this one? Vivien, are you seeing this aura? It looks like someone set her soul on fire."

"No," Vivien said. "Sorry, Julia. I still can't see auras like you. I see hints of a little cloudiness but not a storm."

Julia frowned. "It seems like that gift should have kicked in more for you already."

"May I tell her what's happening?" Vivien asked Nina.

Nina started to speak but then merely nodded.

"This is Nina Cole. She escaped a serial killer sixteen months ago and is his only survivor. She needs our help finding peace for the six who did not make it," Vivien explained. "We think they might be influencing people around her."

"And the killer is not dead, is he?" Julia concluded with a nod. "That explains the murky overcoat this one is wearing. She's still marked for death. He's covered her with bad intentions. You're going to need more than a sage bath to get rid of that cosmic stain."

Nina hugged her arms to her waist.

"He's in jail," Jacob asserted. "He can't hurt her."

Julia pressed her lips together with pity. "You're talking to a ghost, but your head is still thinking like the world is only what you can see and touch. Of course, he can still hurt her. He's hurting her now. Trauma lives in the soul. Those scars will always be there."

Nina bit her lip, not speaking.

"Careful. He'll try to sneak into your dreams," Julia warned. "Don't let him live in your head."

Nina could do nothing about the nightmares. Well, sleeping pills, but she didn't want to feel groggy.

"We think maybe his past victims are upset that she survived." Heather made a move to reclaim her spot around the séance circle. "Nina has been having a run of bad luck. She's been affected by living people who don't seem to be acting on their own accord. It could be possessions or ghostly influences. We think the first step is helping the other women move on. There are six of them."

Julia didn't appear happy with the proposed plan. "It's tricky business with one, let alone six. You girls haven't dealt with wronged spirits before, not like this. They're like vortexes, desperately sucking any energy they can. Full of need and desperation and rage. It's unpredictable."

"That's why we called you," Heather said. "I know you want us to do this ourselves, to use the book and the magic you gave us but this—"

"Not with this," Julia interjected. "I don't know that I would have attempted this one even when I was at the peak of my power."

"Please help us," Nina begged.

"We can't leave them in limbo." Vivien stood next to Heather and grabbed her hand. "We're doing this. Don't make us do it without you."

Sue and Lorna joined hands.

Nina looked at Jacob. "You don't have to stay."

He frowned. "I'm going to pretend you didn't suggest that."

Jacob took Vivien's hand.

"You're not doing this without me," Julia assured them.

Nina was the last to join hands as she reached for Lorna and Jacob. The energy surged, lifting their hair in a now-familiar reaction.

Julia faded only to reappear next to Heather in her 1920s garb. The youthful spirit whispered in her granddaughter's ear. Heather answered just as quietly. Julia nodded.

"Get ready to do-si-do, promenade, and hold your partners tight, ladies. This is one dance you don't want to misstep." Julia remained between Heather and Vivien. She touched their joined hands and an icy cold shock rushed through the circle. The spirit's body solidified some at the contact until she only had a glimmer of transparency. "They might not all come, but we'll try. Hopefully their connection to the rain cloud is strong enough of a pull. Otherwise, we'll have to take this on the road to where it happened."

Nina was not going back to the scene of the crime. She couldn't.

"Ready?" Heather asked.

When they nodded, Julia said, "I'll lead."

Nina tightened her grip afraid she might be tempted to let go. She told herself to be brave. She needed this to work. So much rode on tonight.

Julia tilted back her head and said, "We open the veil between two worlds to call forth the spirits of Richard Chester Teeter's victims. Come back from the grave so that we may hear. Come back from the grave and show yourself so that we may see. Come back from the grave so that we can guide you to peace. I, Julia Warrick, summon you from beyond. I command you to join us."

The flashing overhead lights popped and went dark.

CHAPTER TWELVE

THE SOFT GLOW of the candles gave little by way of satisfactory light. The shadows they cast flickered ominously over the gathered faces. Nina trembled so badly she was sure her knees would give out.

She didn't want to be in the dark.

She wanted to run.

She knew she couldn't.

This is where she had to be.

"Where are they?" she whispered. Each second felt like an eternity of waiting. "What's happening?"

No one answered.

Nina felt a tear slip over her cheek, but she couldn't brush it away. Lorna and Jacob gripped her hands. She felt the others trying to give her their strength, and in return, she tried to keep her fear from radiating back at them.

It didn't work. The terror built inside of her.

I can't be here. I can't be here. Please. I can't—

Gray lights began to move over the séance cloth. Bare feet appeared, first one pair, then another, then a third. The lights climbed slower than they had with Ester, as if they struggled to emerge. One of the pairs disappeared.

"Join us," Julia ordered.

At the firm tone, the feet reemerged to join the others. A fourth pair followed.

Nina remembered the feel of concrete against her feet, bruising and cutting as she ran over the dirty sidewalks.

Legs grew from the ground before becoming hidden by pale blue hospital gowns. A fifth pair started to join them.

"Five," Lorna whispered.

"Come on, ladies, we need six," Vivien urged. "You can do it."

"Join us," Julia said, softer than before.

The first woman formed. Her long dark hair hung limp around her head. Dark circles formed under milky eyes. Her arms hung at her sides.

"April," Nina said, recognizing the woman from

the pictures in the DA's office. She'd been made to stare at them, trying to place if their paths had overlapped. "Number three."

"Six," Lorna stated.

Nina looked but didn't see the faint lights right away. They were dimmer than the others.

"We got all six," Lorna said.

A blonde with dark roots manifested. Tattoos ran up her arm, under the sleeve of her gown, and then reappeared on her neck.

"Vicky," Nina said. "She's the only blonde."

The third appeared, much in the same state. A chuck of her curly hair had noticeably been cut off.

"Gemma Ridges," Jacob said.

The fourth, a curvy woman with a nose piercing, had a gown that seemed to give off the impression of smoke without flames.

"Cady." Nina glanced at Jacob, who nodded in confirmation.

The fifth had long, black hair that fell in front of her face. Her gown was torn.

"Maria Diaz," Jacob said.

The sixth still struggled as she displayed one foot.

"That will be Nancy. She was number six." Nina had seen Nancy when she was still alive.

The ghosts wore hospital gowns and appeared in varying states of torment. They stood rooted against the cloth within the circle of symbols. Their arms didn't move except for the occasional twitch of a hand.

Nina couldn't stop her tears. She took several deep breaths. As a soft sob escaped her, the ghosts turned their attention toward her, rotating so they all faced her—except for Nancy's single foot.

"Spirits you have been found pure. We release you into the light. Go in peace and love," Heather said.

A couple of them flickered but didn't leave.

Julia looked at her granddaughter and arched a brow.

Heather gave a small shrug at the censure. "It was worth a try."

"We're here to help you," Julia said. "We're here to listen. Tell us what you need to find peace."

They continued to stare at Nina.

"I'm sorry," Nina whispered. "I'm sorry all of this happened to you. I'm sorry I couldn't..."

"He's caught," Jacob said.

"Yes." Nina nodded. "That bastard is in jail. He'll never hurt anyone again. Everyone will know what he is. You don't have to stay. I promise I'll make sure he never gets out. I'll tell them."

Nina didn't want to talk about it, but she realized it wasn't just about her experience. She had to speak for all of them. She was the only one who could.

"Yellow," April whispered. "Tall."

"Tall and yellow?" Jacob repeated. "What does that mean?"

"Shh, handsome, let them talk," Julia ordered. "Go on, love."

"Home," April said.

"Barn," Cady added, her tone raspier. "Yellow."

"Home," April repeated.

Each word felt as if it pulled something from inside of Nina. She felt them using her, draining her energy.

"Is the yellow barn your home?" Lorna asked.

April appeared to grow angry and shouted, "Yellow!"

"I don't think so," Sue whispered.

"Go on," Julia encouraged.

"Find," Cady said.

"Route Four," April's complexion cleared some. "Take us home."

"Tall, yellow barn off Route Four?" Jacob asked. "Is that where you are?"

"Find," Cady repeated.

"We will," he promised. "I'll tell the DA first thing in the morning. We'll bring you home. We won't stop looking until we find you."

April's body erupted into bright lights and danced over their heads before disappearing. Nina felt the woman's release, as well as the lingering pain she left behind.

"Cady, how can we help you?" Vivien asked, singling the ghost out. The direct question appeared to help the spirit focus.

"Tell him I didn't want to leave," Cady said, still staring at Nina. "Tell him I love him."

Nina felt lightheaded as Cady sapped energy from her. They said spirits had to get energy from somewhere. With the lights out, it looked like they'd chosen her to be their source. Nina didn't fight it. She let them take whatever she had to give.

Nina looked at Cady's hand and saw a wedding ring. "Your husband?"

"Tell him I love him," Cady repeated.

"I will," Nina promised.

Cady followed April, swirling into lights overhead before vanishing. Again, she felt the woman's release followed by the lingering of her fear.

"Maria?" Nina started to fall and caught herself. "What can we do for you?"

"Something isn't right," Julia said. "They need too much. Who the blazes let you—?"

Julia disappeared.

"Grandma?" Heather called, looking around. "Julia?"

They all searched the stage, craning their necks.

"She's gone," Heather said.

"What happened?" Vivien asked.

"I don't know," Heather said. "I think it was too much for her. We have to keep going."

"I feel dizzy." Nina fought to keep her eyes open even as her vision blurred. "Can I sit down?"

"Don't let go," Vivien ordered the others. "Send everything you got at Nina. They're using her to manifest."

Nina felt them bolstering her and her legs stopped shaking and her vision cleared. Maria had not answered, so she tried, "Gemma? Can you talk to us?"

Gemma began to rock, shaking her head. "No. No. No..."

She kept repeating the word.

"Vicky?" Nina asked.

Vicky's mouth opened as if she would bite something. Her teeth clamped down. Her chest began to heave and red filled her body as rage emanated from her. "Balls."

"What balls?" Vivien asked.

Vicky became less transparent. She took a step toward Nina. Her eyes narrowed in anger and her entire body shook. Thankfully, the barrier of symbols stopped her from leaving the séance area. "You knee that son of a bitch Viper in the balls for leaving me in that bar. He set me up."

"Oh, I got that one, sweetheart," Vivien offered. "Don't you worry."

"Asshole," Vicky grumbled. She exploded more than floated away.

"Are you really going to...?" Sue asked.

"Oh, yeah. After the glimpse I just got off of Vicky? You bet I am." Vivien took a deep breath. "That biker bastard has it coming. He sold her to Teeter. Left her drugged and vulnerable."

"Are they moving on?" Nina asked, unsure after Vicky's explosive display.

"No. No. No..." Gemma continued, dropping to the floor to curl into a tight ball. She rolled onto her side.

Maria didn't move, and Nancy didn't fully appear.

"Most of the time people just want to be heard," Heather said. "After they die, they sometimes need help with that. If they need us to do something, we'll do it for them. But if they won't tell us..."

"What do we do with these three?" Sue asked. "We can't leave them like this, and we can't send them back to suffer."

"Maria?" Nina tried again. She understood how the spirits might feel. There had been times when Nina had been locked in a terrible moment, scared to do so much as breathe. "Can you hear me?"

Maria's hand twitched, but she didn't move.

"It's over. He can't hurt us," Nina said. "I promise you I'll make sure everyone knows what he did. I'll testify. I'll speak for us. I won't stop until all of you are home."

Maria didn't move.

"Spirit you're pure. Ah?" Nina tried to remember the words.

"Spirit you have been found pure," Heather said for her. "We release you into the light. Go in peace and love."

Maria's head lifted, and she smiled faintly before looking toward the ceiling. Her body dissolved into embers reaching for the sky.

"No. No. No..." Gemma started to fade.

Nina broke contact with the others and dropped to the stage.

"Nina, no!" Vivien ordered, but it was too late.

Nina placed her hands on the cloth and leaned over to see Gemma's face as she lay on the floor. The ghost hugged her legs, and tear trails stained her cheeks. The sound of a shovel hitting dirt echoed, and Gemma jerked violently.

"Nina, don't," Lorna warned.

"Be careful," Jacob urged.

"Gemma?" Nina didn't think as she reached for the ghost. She couldn't let the spirit fade. She couldn't leave her like this. "Gemma, look at me."

"No. No. No—"

"Let me carry it for you." Her hand touched the icy cold form of the spirit.

Gemma stopped talking. Nina felt the all too familiar fear and dread working up her arm encased in an icy chill.

"Hey, Gemma," Nina soothed. "You don't have to stay here. You can leave."

"Shh," Gemma insisted, eyes wide in panic.

"It's okay," Nina whispered. "He can't find you. Not here. Not ever."

Gemma's hand stretched toward her. The ghost

touched her face. Suddenly, a cold rush swooshed into Nina as Gemma dove into her body.

"Nina!" Jacob cried out.

Nina felt Gemma trying to hide. She fell to the floor, unable to move. Someone tugged her foot, pulling her out of the circle.

"Nina, come on," Jacob urged. He crawled over her, touching her face. "Look at me. Nina, please."

Nina knew Gemma's pain, knew how hard it was to see past it. When something bad happened, people became burdened with the memory. When something terrible happened, they became locked in a dark place. Gemma had plunged past that darkness to become petrified.

Jacob's touch and soothing voice calmed Nina, and in turn that feeling radiated into Gemma. The spirit released its tight grip. Nina felt her leaving. The spirit pulled out of her and rose past Jacob.

Nina shivered violently. Jacob pulled her into his arms, holding her. He rubbed her back, trying to give her his heat.

"Nancy," Nina insisted when she could move. She pushed at his chest. There was one left. She needed to finish this.

The others stood in their places, watching. Nina

had broken the circle, and so they waited with unjoined hands.

Nina somehow managed to get to her feet with Jacob's help. She held her hand toward Lorna. "Let's finish this."

They joined hands. Nina concentrated on Nancy's feet.

"Come on, Nancy, join us," Heather urged.

Nina breathed hard. Gemma had taken a lot out of her. They all had. She focused on staying upright.

Nancy struggled to appear.

A dull ache thumped behind Nina's right eye. She wanted this to be over. She felt the others trying to send her their energy and support, but her senses had started to dull. Gemma's feelings lingered like icicles that wouldn't thaw.

The last ghost formed. Her image grew from the ground. The tiny lights swirled, some extinguishing before making it to the top. Nancy struggled to take shape.

The hospital gown appeared to be mint green, though it was difficult to be sure with the transparency of the image. The gown didn't match the others. The light moved up the chest and down the arms before finally illuminating red hair.

"This isn't right," Nina said. "I don't understand.

The woman turned to look at her.

"That's not Nancy." Nina looked at Jacob for confirmation. "Who is that?"

Jacob shook his head. "I have no clue."

"There were seven of us, right?" Nina asked needlessly. She knew the answer. She'd seen the evidence they'd found. She was unlucky number seven.

The candles flared. It reflected into the bodies of two more women in gowns.

"Oh, shit," Vivien swore. "Lorna, the cloth."

Nina glanced down. The séance cloth was wrinkled where she'd crawled onto it, folding over some of the symbols.

Suddenly, lights shot off the candles, no longer confined to the cloth. The hundreds of tiny lights became thousands, scattering like fireflies. Ghosts appeared behind Heather and close to Lorna. They spread out over the stage, spilling into the seating below.

"Six, nine," Lorna counted, trying to keep up. "Um, twelve."

Vivien and Heather released their hands. They rushed around the circle, gathering everyone together.

Nina released Lorna but kept hold of Jacob.

Tears spilled from her eyes. "There are so many of us."

"Fifteen," Lorna said.

"Nancy," Jacob pointed down to the floor. Nina followed his finger to find Nancy wearing pale blue.

Seven ladies wore the mint green, and seven wore burgundy gowns.

"How did we miss this?" Jacob said, more to himself than to the others. He counted silently to himself, before saying, "Twenty-one victims?"

"That's a lot of ghosts," Sue whispered. "We can't do them at once."

Nina wasn't sure how she could help them all move on. The first five had taken so much out of her. The ghosts became brighter. She felt them taking from her, forcing her to take from Jacob through their connection. His face began to pale, and his breathing became labored. At this rate, the ghosts would kill them both. Already Nina was tapped.

She pulled her hand from Jacob's and began walking through the spirits, away from him.

"Nina, don't," Jacob tried to follow, but the ghosts blocked his path.

Nina saw their faces, eyes watching her. She felt their pain, knew it so well.

"Let's try to send them on," Vivien said.

"Spirits you have been found pure," the other women said in unison. "We release you into the light. Go in peace and love."

The spirits didn't move.

"Why did that stop working?" Sue asked. "Normally, we can get at least a few to take us up on the offer."

"They're not ready to leave," Heather said. "They have unfinished business."

"We can't keep this up. Maybe we try again later. Give Nina a break," Jacob said. He made a move to come to her, but she had put distance between them, and the ghosts refused to let him pass.

Nina crossed the stage, feeling them around her. The air became colder, but she ignored it. Some appeared confused, others angry, and still others incoherent. The ghosts began to follow her. With each step she weakened, but how could she deny them her energy?

"Nina," Jacob called after her. "Come back this way."

She heard his footsteps weaving and stopping as if he tried to get to her.

She looked at the victim's faces, wondering what she would want someone to say if she were in their place. Sympathy? Anger? Promises?

"He's going to pay," Nina managed as she fell to her hands and knees.

Thud. Pain radiated from the hard landing.

She felt more than saw the spirits coming toward her.

"Nina," Jacob yelled.

Her vision dimmed. She couldn't fight. Her hands slipped from under her as she fell to the floor. Before she passed out, she watched as a sea of ghostly feet faded into black.

CHAPTER THIRTEEN

NINA RECOGNIZED THIS PLACE. She'd been trapped here many times, reliving the moments as if they first happened. She tried to fight it, but her body was weak, and the pull too strong. There was no choice but to push open that restaurant door and walk. She stepped into her past.

Nina tried to tally how many drinks she'd had but kept coming back to the number one. One glass of wine that she hadn't even finished. The waiter had insisted she try it with the steak, and her coworkers had seconded the motion. It was fine, but not for her.

So why did she feel wobbly?

Why were her legs turning into jelly beneath her?

The dinners were really an excuse for the bus drivers to get together and swap stories from the road. Normally, she would walk home afterward. It was only a few blocks.

Tonight, she could barely make her feet work.

"Ride, ma'am?"

Nina looked up from her blurry feet at the question. She tried to answer, but her mouth felt numb, and only a gurgle of noise passed her lips.

"I got ya," the man insisted. "Good thing you called."

Nina felt her legs give out from under her, and the man propped her up. Her shoes skidded on the sidewalk as she was pushed into the backseat of a car. The vinyl seat stuck to her cheek. She tried to tell him she hadn't called for a ride. She tried to push herself up. Nothing worked.

A shadowy head loomed from the front. "You really should take it easy on the red meat. Don't you know steaks will kill you? Good thing I'm a doctor. I can help you with that."

He laughed like he'd just said the funniest thing in the world.

Her vision dimmed, going black. It only felt like an instant, but when she managed to open her eyes, she was on her back, being wheeled through crumbling concrete halls. The metal beneath her body made for a hard bed. She saw graffiti, unreadable names and gang tags in bold, intertwined letters. Eventually, she passed the number seven with a pair of wings.

She moaned, trying to form words.

Who was rolling the cart? Where was she?

Whatever drugs were in her system kept her from becoming too alert. The ride felt like it took hours, but she couldn't be sure as she drifted in and out of consciousness. Nina summoned every bit of strength she had and tried to lift her hands, but something kept them locked at her sides. She tried to reach for a doorway, hoping to stop their progress but her fingers merely grazed the hard-textured wall. The tips stung and bled from the contact.

"Don't you worry. It'll be your turn soon enough, patient number seven," the male voice said. "I'm Dr. Teeter. I'll be taking care of you."

Doctor?

Why did she need a doctor?

Nothing made sense. The dirtiness of the room contrasted with the pungent odor of sterilization. It smelled like industrial cleaners had been poured all around. They wet her body, causing thin material to cling to her in discomfort. Everything itched. The old lightbulb on a string of wires gave off an awful, constant hum. Tears rolled down her temples.

Often, Dr. Teeter was there, talking. His words made little sense.

Sometimes his words were directed at her, "You're very special, Seven. You will complete my cycle of transformation and make me powerful. Did you know that some cultures believe you can consume the power of your enemies? But they have it wrong. It just can't be anyone, anytime. It takes a lot of work to get there. All parties must be willing. You're not now, but you will be. You must feed energy to create energy. That is why you must be connected to the six that came before. Don't worry, though. It will be your turn soon."

Sometimes his words were mumbled to himself, "I don't need their approval. I am more of a doctor than they will ever be. This is my destiny. Hacks."

Sometimes his words were gleeful and far away, "Oh, don't leave yet my little plaything. We're not done. Sing for me, my angel."

Always they were delusional, "Bow before your god, or I will destroy you with my greatness."

In response to all this, Nina could only manage gurgled mutterings and hazy glares.

Time itself lost meaning. She felt sharp pains as she was injected with something. Her thoughts and dreams alternated between loud, piercing screams and deafening silence. The metal bed moved, tilting forward so that she half hung, half stood upright.

Whenever she opened her eyes, she expected —*hoped*—to be home. But each time, she was flung deeper into the pits of utter despair. She lived in constant fear. Sometimes she was on her stomach, on her back, hanging upside down on the tilted bed. At intervals, she felt as if she floated above herself. And then she discovered where the other screams were coming from, and that is when she learned the true definition of hell.

Part of her believed it was because she wished it so badly that the thought of escape was so emblazoned behind every thought that she willed the opportunity into existence. Or maybe she had been so focused that she saw it when it came. The strap from her wrist restraint had worn through from the constant movement against metal, and she managed to snap her arm free. Tiny locks held the restraints against her wrists, ankles, and waist. She couldn't pry them open.

Surgical tools had been placed next to her, lined up on a blue cloth. The display was angled so that she'd been able to stare at the tools for hours, imagining the worst. Which, truth be told, wasn't as bad as what he likely had planned for her.

Nina fumbled for the scalpel and used it to saw herself free. Everything hurt as she stood. The change in position caused a wave of dizziness. She felt the concrete against her feet as she stumbled and held herself upright.

Gripping the scalpel, she went to where she'd heard the screams, whispering, "I'm coming. I'm coming."

Nina found a prison much like hers. She rushed to cut the woman free, only to realize she was too late. The shock of cold skin caused her to drop her weapon. It clattered somewhere on the shadowed floor.

"I'm sorry. I'm sorry." Nina stumbled for the door, pushing off walls and propelling herself mindlessly forward. All she knew was she needed to keep running, past the spray-painted seven with wings, through the dark tunnels with the damp floor, and finally up narrow steps. She threw herself against a wooden door, slipping in a puddle gathered along the bottom edge as the rain came from the other side. She bruised her shoulder with the force of her hits until the door lifted from its hinges.

Nina pushed into the rain-soaked night, not stopping for anything.

CHAPTER FOURTEEN

EVERYTHING ACHED. The dull lethargy felt like a virus had taken over her body. For a moment, she thought about trying to go back to sleep, but then she remembered where sleep had taken her—back to the nightmare of her ordeal.

Nina expected hospital lights when she opened her eyes. That is where she had been before, with real doctors and nurses trying to keep her calm. She fought their tests and begged them not to drug and restrain her. But then Jacob came, and things calmed. He untied her hands and sat with her as the drugs wore off. He talked to her about everyday things and asked her about her life. He banished the nurses from her room. And those eyes, the soft caring eyes that let her know everything was going to be okay—somehow, someway.

Nina's head was clear, but she struggled to see. A lamp on a bedside table came into slow focus.

Not a hospital.

Not Teeter.

That time had passed. She'd lived through it. The pain of the passing spirits must have thrust her back into the nightmare. Even now, their desperation and panic lingered inside her where they'd touched.

She moaned softly, stirring on a soft mattress. An unfamiliar frosted glass partition acted as a wall. Shadows and light came from the other side.

She turned on the mattress, pushing up to figure out what was happening. The queen-size bed was next to a dresser. The partition didn't block much, and she could see beyond the bedroom. A living room led to a railing that would usually line the stairs leading down. Beyond that was an old apothecary cabinet.

Sue's house? She couldn't think of anywhere else she'd be.

What had happened after the séance? She remembered ghosts, so many lost souls. She remembered falling and then...the nightmare.

Nina slid her feet off the bed. She wore the same

clothes as during the séance, but her feet were bare. When she tried to stand, lightheadedness slowed her down. It felt like a drop in blood pressure from having laid down for too long rather than a drugged state.

She looked for her phone, automatically wanting to check to see if there was any news on Teeter. She didn't see the device where she usually would have kept it on the nightside table.

Going toward the living room, she found a built-in bookshelf on one side and, on the other, an island and barstools that created a boundary to the kitchen. A small table next to a window could have been the dining area. There were no secrets in the floor plan. She glanced around the glass partition and found a bathroom with a door to indicate there was at least one private place in the studio apartment.

Reclaimed wood furniture gave a rustic feel as it was backdropped against an exposed brick wall. Faded white paint spelled, "*Warrick*," on the red brick. The faint sound of traffic hummed through the window.

Warrick? As in Julia Warrick? Was this part of the theater?

Seeing the back of the couch, she pushed off the partition wall and aimed for it, wobbling as she tried to control her dizziness. She gripped the back and moved to sit down. Seeing feet, she stopped short of sitting on them.

"Oh!" Nina said in surprise to find Jacob sleeping on the couch. He didn't wear a shirt, and a blanket was tossed over his stomach.

She started to back away to let him sleep.

His eyes opened, and he blinked several times before focusing on her. A smile crossed his lips, and he suppressed a yawn as he said, "Hey, you're awake. How do you feel?"

"Where are we?" Nina tried to look anywhere but at him. She wasn't thinking clearly in her light-headed state but staring at his chest didn't seem like a good plan. It had become difficult enough to resist her feelings for him.

How long had it been since she'd had sex? It was before her abduction, so almost two years?

"Apartment above the theater," he answered, not seeming to notice her internal struggle. "Everyone thought it would be best to bring you up here where we could keep an eye on you. The building has protection built in by Julia. I honestly can't say I understood it all, but after you passed out, we thought... Do you remember passing out?"

Nina nodded. She heard him shift on the couch and imagined the blanket sliding down his stomach.

"Do you remember the ghosts?" he asked.

Nina shivered and rubbed her arms. "Yes."

Yes, she remembered. Their feelings lingered inside of her like the echo of a hangover.

"Heather said that they drained your energy, and that's why you've been asleep for three days. They didn't let us near until they took all they could. They were fighting for you to hear them, but there were too many."

Nina frowned. Three days?

He continued, "I guess, normally—*if you can call any of this normal*—they take from everyone, but the spirits felt a connection to you after what you'd been through. So, they psychically attached to you to manifest. Lorna has been feeding you energy slowly to bring you back."

At that, she finally looked at him. "Feeding me energy? What does that mean?"

"Since she's a healer, she was able to use me to help you. Let's just say the two of us have been sleeping in quite a bit." He rubbed the back of his head. "Coffee? I can make some. Sue brought groceries for when you woke up."

Nina thought about offering to do it, but she

needed to sit down. So instead, she nodded and went to a barstool by the kitchen island. Jacob tossed the blankets off his lap. He wore green cutoff sweatpants and nothing else. An open duffle bag showed he'd brought his luggage.

Seeing her looking at the bag, he said, "I checked out of the hotel."

"To babysit me?" Nina caught herself glancing at his chest.

"I wouldn't call it babysitting." Jacob crossed to the kitchen and pulled ground coffee out of a cabinet. "Lorna brought some of your clothes. They're in the bedroom dresser."

And now she stared at his naked back.

Strong muscles mesmerized her as she watched them move. Her libido kicked into overdrive. Never had making coffee looked so sexy.

"Do you think you can eat something?" He glanced back at her.

When their eyes met, she became flustered and could only manage a nod. She wasn't really hungry for food.

He arched a brow but turned back to what he was doing. He pulled two mugs out of a cabinet and creamer from the fridge.

"You know your way around," Nina observed. She stared at her hands.

"After three days, I should." He poured creamer into one of the mugs. "There's no television so it was either read, explore, watch my tablet, or stare at you sleep."

Nina laughed. "Oh, great. That's only mildly embarrassing."

"I'd use the word adorable," he admitted.

Nina purposefully kept her gaze on her hands as she threaded and unthreaded her fingers. "What happened to the others after I passed out?"

"They've come by to check on you when they can. I have their numbers to call if anything changes."

He didn't make a move to do that as he put an empty mug under the coffee pot stream and poured what had been brewed into the cup with the creamer.

"Sue had to open her bookstore for an online event. Influencers were coming by. Heather is trying to get some rental options ready for you, though she said you could have this one if you want it. Lorna," he slid the coffee in front of her, "comes up from running the theater every few hours to check on you. She feeds you my energy or gives me your tiredness, depending on how you look at the transfer. And Vivien said something about meetings, but then I learned she took a road trip to knee that biker in the balls as promised. She also turned his name over to Delany with an anonymous tip and a screenshot of messages from his phone."

"I meant the *other* women," Nina clarified. "The ghosts."

"Oh, yes, of course." He inhaled a deep breath and held it a few seconds before letting go. "I called Delany and told her about the yellow barn on Route Four. They managed to locate it and have a forensic team out there. She wanted to know where I got the information. I told her I had a confidential source, but I don't think she's going to let it go if they find any evidence. I also told her I believed there were more victims than we previously thought. I'm still trying to figure out how to explain the intel. I can't exactly tell her we got it from a séance."

"Tell her I remembered something," Nina answered. "Tell her you got it from me. I have to testify anyway. I'll say my memory is coming back from that night."

"Is it?"

"In pieces," she nodded. "I'll tell him I remembered Teeter bragging about it. They can't prove that he wasn't. He talked nonstop. It's believable."

"I don't want to ask you to lie under oath," he said. "You have enough pressure on you."

Nina wrapped her fingers around the mug. Heat worked its way over her hands. "I think in this case lying is for the greater good. They'll laugh us out of court if we mention ghosts, psychics, or séances. I'm not going to risk him getting out, and I'm not going to turn the trial into any more of a media circus than it will already be."

"I don't like it, but fine. If Delany presses, I'll tell her I got the information from you." Jacob pulled the mug out from under the coffee stream and replaced it with the carafe.

"Did their spirits move on?" Nina forced herself to take a drink. Her throat was a little dry, and the heat felt great as it stung its way down.

"No, I don't think so. I'm sorry. They faded when you passed out." He leaned against the island. His hand wrapped around his mug as he looked at her. "We thought it best not to try again while you were sleeping. Lorna didn't say, but I think they almost killed you."

The steadiness of his eyes and the nearness of his naked chest made it difficult to concentrate. Her ring hand tingled with the now familiar magic as if wanting to tell her something. She didn't need a ring, or magic, to tell her about her connection to Jacob. That invisible thread had been sewing itself between them from that first moment.

All the moments between them filtered through her thoughts. She saw his eyes becoming clear in the hospital, and his hands as he escorted her home. His distorted face as it appeared through a peephole when she looked out of her front door.

"I'm not ashamed to admit it terrified me to see you like that," he confessed.

Nina pushed up from her barstool and went around the island to his side.

"You should sit," he said. "I'll get you whatever you want—"

Nina stopped his words by placing her hands on his face. Breathing heavily, she glanced at his mouth and then his eyes. He didn't resist.

She pulled him to her and kissed him. She'd been wanting to do that for a long time. His lips were warm, and he parted them to deepen the contact. A small moan sounded in the back of his throat. It fueled her simmering desire for him.

His arms wrapped around her waist, pulling her tight against him. The feel of his chest against hers sent a shock of awareness through her. It had been so long since she'd been held.

Her hands became desperate, running along his arms and neck. He gripped her ass and rocked into her before reaching for a breast. His hand seemed to be everywhere at once.

The months of resisting her feelings exploded into a powerful force. It brought them together, almost as if destiny were out of their control. This moment was meant to be. She wanted him, desperately, entirely, *now*.

His hands moved around to her fly. He unbuttoned her jeans. She fell back against the island to allow him access. His eyes stayed on hers, the intensity stating all the things he didn't say. He wanted her just as badly as she wanted him.

Nina felt the rough material of her jeans sliding down her hips. She stepped on the legs to pull them off all the way. She slid them aside as she grabbed for his waistband. Her hand moved beneath the soft material to find his aroused length. She rubbed her thigh against his in invitation.

Jacob again grabbed her ass and lifted her off the floor. Laughter bubbled up from deep inside. Her legs wrapped around his waist as he carried her toward the couch. He placed her on the cushions. She fell onto her back, pulling him with her.

The connection between them deepened. She had no way of telling if it was magically induced, but she treasured the feeling. He resumed kissing her as his hips settled between her legs.

Nina gasped as he entered her. Their breaths crashed together in the kiss. It felt so much deeper than two bodies frantically joining. She felt him in her soul.

They met in perfect rhythm. As the pleasure built inside, her climax came too quickly. She wanted time to stop so she could thoroughly feel each second.

Suddenly, Jacob stiffened and stopped moving. She kept rocking into him, searching for that final surge of gratification. At first, she thought he'd climaxed, but after a few seconds, she pressed her head back to look at him. His face was frozen like a human statue.

"Jacob?" she asked, slapping his arm. His eyes were partially closed, and his arousal remained hard inside her.

The need to finish drove her hips to adjust beneath him. She climaxed, crying out in surprise as she tried to reason what was going on.

"Nina? Is that you? Are you awake?" Lorna's voice preceded her fast footfall coming up the steps.

"Don't look," Nina shouted.

The steps stopped. "What's going on?"

"Don't..." Nina was trapped beneath Jacob's form. She didn't know what to do. "Ah, shit, something is wrong."

"What's—*oh, my god, I'm sorry!*"

"Lorna," Nina hesitated, trying to find the right words. "Shit. Shit. I need your help. Something's wrong with Jacob."

"Uh?" Lorna's footfall came closer, much slower than before. "What seems to be the...? Is he...?"

"Frozen, or something," Nina answered. She slapped his arm and angled her head to try to see the woman. "I don't know what happened."

Lorna covered her mouth as if trying not to laugh. "I think I might."

"What?"

"I think we just discovered what your power might be." Lorna turned away, and her shoulders shook with contained laughter.

"I did this?" Nina pressed her head back to see Jacob's face. His eyes hadn't moved, and his lips and tongue remained locked in mid-kiss.

"That's one way of making it last longer," Lorna managed, snickering.

"This isn't funny. What do I do?"

"Just let me get out of here. Then focus your thoughts on undoing it. I'll give you twenty minutes before I come back up." Lorna's feet rushed down the stairs, and she firmly shut a door to mark her exit.

"Jacob," Nina whispered, staring at him. She thought of her tingling hand and tried to push that magical feeling into him. "Wake up."

Suddenly, he pushed forward, softly crying out his release.

Nina watched his face, stunned that it had worked.

He grinned down at her, breathing hard.

Nina returned the smile and pretended like nothing strange had happened. What else could she do?

"I don't want this moment to end," he admitted. "I've thought about it for a long time."

Nina couldn't hold back a small laugh at that.

Jacob sat back. "Did I say something funny?"

Nina sat up on the couch. She reached for him, touching his neck. "No. You said something perfect."

CHAPTER FIFTEEN

"WE GOT PROBLEMS, Lorna. Something big is going on."

Nina didn't recognize the woman's muffled voice coming from the bottom of the stairs.

Jacob was in the process of making them sandwiches and set a jar of mayo down on the island. "Do you know who that is?"

Nina shook her head and went toward the stairwell. She'd already pulled on her jeans in anticipation of Lorna rejoining them. The door at the bottom of the stairs was cracked open, and the voice carried.

"I don't know what happened, but I was on the shuttle with Angel and Constance. Suddenly, everyone stopped moving. Thankfully the bus stopped moving too. It felt like magic, but it didn't come from me. I teleported here as fast as I could find a private—"

Nina opened the door at the bottom of the stairs. The woman instantly stopped talking. Her curly hair was piled on the top of her head, held back with a kitten ears headband. She wore shorts and a theme park t-shirt.

"Kari, this is Nina Cole," Lorna introduced. "Nina, Kari Grove."

"Hi," Nina said.

Kari's gaze went to Nina's ring, and she visibly relaxed. "Okay, it's starting to make sense now. We have another one?"

Lorna nodded. "Yes."

"Why didn't you call me?" Kari asked. "How far along are things? Does she...?"

"She knows," Nina answered for Lorna.

"You guys were taking Constance to Orlando," Lorna said. "We didn't want to interrupt. It's all she could talk about for months, and to be honest, it has been wonderful hearing her sound like a kid after all that happened to her. We got this."

"So, this is handled?" Kari insisted. "Because I should get back. They think I'm in the restroom, and I don't want someone trying to come in my stall thinking it's empty."

Lorna nodded. "Go. Call us later."

Kari smiled at her. "Nice to meet you, Nina."

"Nice to—"

Kari disappeared before Nina could finish her sentence.

"Did she just...?" Jacob slowly came down the steps. Nina had forgotten for a moment that he might be behind her.

"Yeah," Lorna said. "That's Kari. She's one of Julia's wards. We helped her...well, that's a long, weird story. Her gift is teleporting. We'll call her back if we need her."

"Are there a lot of you?" Jacob asked. "I guess I assumed everyone was at the thing the other night."

"Just us and Kari. Nina is number six to find a ring, well, seven if you count Julia the original owner. We've helped many others, like you, of course, but only six rings." Lorna motioned toward the stairs. "Shall we go upstairs? Vivien and Heather are getting tacos. Sue will join us as soon as she closes the shop. Today is the last day for the social media video shoots."

"I was about to make sandwiches," Jacob said, leading the way back to the apartment.

"If you must, but these tacos are life changing," Lorna said. "There is this food truck down by the beach that literally may be the concession stand to heaven."

"Nina hasn't eaten for three days." Jacob stopped on the stairs and looked down at her in worry.

"Oddly, I don't feel starved," Nina told him.

"That's because Jacob has been eating for two." Lorna gestured that they should keep walking.

"That makes me sound pregnant," Jacob grumbled, resuming his climb.

Nina didn't follow him as she leaned down to glance into the theater lobby, looking for a sign of something paranormal.

"You won't see them without a séance," Lorna said as if reading her thoughts. "I don't think they're still here."

"We have to help them," Nina said, knowing the toll helping five of the women had taken on her. By her calculation, there were fifteen left of the twenty other victims. "All of them. Whatever it takes."

"We will," Lorna assured her.

"What did Julia say about it when you asked her?" Nina asked. "Did she have any ideas on how to handle this?"

Lorna frowned and glanced behind her toward the lobby. "Julia hasn't reappeared yet. The séance took its toll on everyone. I'm sure she just needs more time to recover. She'll go to Heather when she's able."

Nina could see that Lorna was trying not to worry her, but the stress was there behind the woman's gaze.

"For now, you should take it easy," Lorna insisted. "I've never seen that bad of a reaction to a séance. Had we known we were dealing with twenty and not six, we would have handled it differently. Please don't think we were neglectful by not taking you to a hospital. It's just we could help you more here."

"I don't think that. I appreciate not having a three-day hospital bill, and I'm not really a fan of doctors. I know you did everything you could. I should have listened to you and consumed more sugar. Next time I will." Nina started to climb, only to stop. "Um, listen. About..."

Nina pointed upward toward the couch.

"Consider your secret safe." Lorna grinned. She rubbed her bent knee. "When I called to tell Vivien and Heather that you were awake, I only said we learned your special skill. I didn't tell them what was going on when it activated."

Nina swallowed back her embarrassment. "Thanks."

"No problem." Lorna again motioned that they should go upstairs. "I must admit Vivien would *love* that story. Don't be surprised if she knows you two took it to the next level when she sees you. It's hard to keep secrets from her."

"I've noticed that." Nina finished climbing the stairs. She found Jacob in the kitchen, putting away the sandwich supplies.

"It's hard for a man to compete with life changing tacos," he explained when he caught her watching.

"That might be the truest sentence ever uttered," Lorna chuckled. "Before I forget, William wanted me to invite you to join their poker game tonight if you want a break from all the girls."

"William?" Nina asked.

"Heather's brother, my man." Lorna grinned. "He came by a few days ago to bring me lunch and met Jacob."

"Thank him for me," Jacob said, "but perhaps another time would be best. I think I need to be here right now."

"To take care of Nina?" Lorna nodded in under-standing. "That's so romantic."

"No," Jacob shook his head.

Nina looked at him, confused.

"To try these tacos." He winked at her.

Nina laughed. "I hope all this buildup isn't too much hype for them to live up to."

"Oh, it's not," Lorna assured them.

They fell into silence. Jacob busied himself wiping down the counters even though they didn't need it.

Nina looked around the apartment. "This is nice. I had no idea anything was even up here."

"Isn't it?" Lorna agreed. "I used to live here when I first moved to Freewild Cove. Then Sue before she moved in with Jameson. If you like it, I'm sure Heather will be fine with you living here too."

"I was a little weirded out the first couple of nights," Jacob admitted. "After what happened downstairs, every tiny noise woke me up."

"I always think of this apartment more like a safe house. Downtown location means there's regular cop traffic on the streets at night. The theater has security doors and cameras. When we're not séancing, Julia keeps the paranormal population in line. Oh, and," Lorna pointed toward the bedroom, "there's a fire ladder under the bed if you need to get out in a hurry. Heather had asked me to tell you that, Jacob, but I forgot. There were some fires in town several years back, and she's adamant about fire safety."

"It could do with a television," Jacob said. "Not that I mind the reading selection."

"I suppose," Lorna agreed. "Though you're welcome to sneak down and watch any of the performances or movies. Starting next week, we're doing an ode to the 80s."

A phone began ringing, and Jacob instantly moved toward his duffel bag to answer it. "Excuse me, ladies."

"No worries," Lorna said.

He ducked toward the bedroom. "Hey, yes, I'm here."

"He hasn't left this theater except to run to the hotel to grab his bags," Lorna whispered. "He's barely left this apartment."

"He's a good man," Nina said.

"I think it's a little more than that. He's crazy about you. He's been so worried." Lorna leaned to the side to check on him as if to make sure they couldn't be overheard.

The sound of Jacob's voice came from the bedroom. It was too low to make out what he was saying.

"We met at one of the worst times in my life. I don't think I could have made it without him." Nina leaned forward on the island.

A thud sounded on the steps. Nina jumped a little as she turned her attention.

"We have tacos," Vivien announced as she came up the stairs. She appeared holding two large bags of food and continued, "We have burritos, churros, more tacos, nachos, quesadillas, fish tacos, taquitos, and tacos."

"That's a lot of food," Nina said.

"Is that a question?" Vivien grinned. "Or a challenge?"

"Fish taco please," Lorna said.

More footsteps sounded, and Heather appeared with two additional bags. "I got the cake, ice cream, cinnamon rolls, and oatmeal cookies with raisins."

"Oatmeal cookies with raisins?" Vivien repeated as she pulled out the Mexican food and placed it on the counter.

"They looked good," Heather defended her choice.

"Are you pregnant?" Vivien asked.

"You're hilarious," Heather drawled wryly.

"Fair enough." Vivien tossed a wrapped taco at Lorna. "Nina?"

"Um, a burrito, please?" Nina answered.

"I mean," Vivien whispered. "Any chance you're pregnant? I'm getting this weird...vibe."

Nina felt the color draining from her face. She looked toward where Jacob still talked on the phone. They hadn't used protection. What in the hell had she been thinking? The idea of a baby had never occurred to her.

"I'm joking," Vivien laughed. "Your face, though."

"You're so not funny," Nina muttered.

"You're not pregnant, as far as I can tell. But you should be more careful." Vivien picked up four packages and slid them over to her. "Here, try these to start."

Nina slowly picked up a burrito.

"Good choice," Heather said. "Make sure you try a taco too."

Vivien opened three quesadillas and then presented them with a hand gesture. "Beef, chicken, veggie."

Lorna grabbed a piece of the chicken.

"Sorry about that." Jacob returned to the kitchen. His brow furrowed in worry.

"Everything all right?" Nina asked.

"That was a friend of mine with the forensics lab." He paused to look at the buffet of food laid out. "They found the site near the yellow barn. DNA has been confirmed for Nancy. Three others have been found. More are expected."

Lorna put her quesadilla down. Heather's hands dropped to the counter, still holding the taco. Vivien sighed and bowed her head.

"Good," Lorna whispered. "That's good."

Nina fingered the burrito, feeling it squish beneath her hands. She set it down, not hungry.

"You need to eat, Nina," Vivien said, not looking up. "Even if you don't feel like you want to. It's been three days. You can't help others if you don't take care of yourself."

Nina picked the food back up and took a bite. That was probably the only thing Vivien could have said to make her eat. They had to help the other women. She nodded as she tasted it. "You're right. It's good. Thank you."

Vivien glanced up at her and gave a small nod of approval. "What about you, Jacob? Land or sea?"

"Beef," he said. When she handed it to him, he added, "Thank you."

The enthusiasm for the meal had lessened.

Nina couldn't get the image of all the ghosts out of her head. Teeter was so much worse than she'd known. It didn't feel possible, and yet she'd seen the proof.

"Bitch!" The man's shout drew their collective attention toward the window. The glass shattered under a blur of movement. Nina gasped. Jacob hopped in front of Nina. A rock thudded on the floor before stopping at Vivien's feet.

Heather rushed to look out. "Asshole!"

"Who was it?" Vivien joined Heather.

"Nina, are you okay?" Lorna rubbed her arm.

Nina nodded.

"I don't know. Just some jerk," Heather said. "He ran off like a coward."

"I'll get a broom." Lorna set to work cleaning up the glass. "I don't want anyone cutting themselves."

"I have some boards downstairs." Heather frowned as she examined the broken glass. "I'll put a piece in the window until Sue can come fix it."

Nina picked up a rock from the floor. "Is this another possession?"

"Could be." Heather went down the stairs. "Three years ago, I would have thought it was one of Viv's one-night stands not wanting to let go."

"That only happened twice," Vivien grumbled.

The sound of traffic became louder with the broken window. Nina felt a cool breeze sweeping in. It reminded her of the spirits, of how cold they had been.

"It has to of been one of the ghosts, right?" Nina insisted. "Or several? They're mad that I survived."

"We don't know for sure." Lorna swept the glass into a dustpan.

"It's a rational assumption," Vivien inserted.

"Nancy," Nina reasoned. "She has reason to be upset with me."

She hadn't escaped fast enough to help Nancy.

"Jealousy is an emotion, not a reason," Vivien corrected. "If she's jealous you survived, don't let that guilt hang around your neck. That's not on you."

That was easier said than done.

"Survivor's guilt is a real thing," Jacob said. "It's a very natural reaction to trauma. Do you remember we talked about this?"

They had. At the hospital when they first met.

"I can't change how I feel." Nina tried to take another bite of the food but couldn't make herself eat. She set the burrito down on its wrapper.

Lorna dumped the glass shards into the trash can and washed her hands.

"You accept those feelings," Jacob said. "Share them with the people who care about you. Don't let them fester."

Nina glanced at Lorna and Vivien. She felt a connection to them on a deep and magical level. She felt

Sue down the block and Heather downstairs. There was even a small tug toward the Kari person she'd just met.

Then there was Jacob. She wouldn't call the connection magical, per se. Her connection to him didn't happen when she slipped on a ring. It had grown with time, naturally.

"It helps to do a kindness for others, too," Lorna said between bites of the quesadilla. "Like you're already doing."

"Eat," Vivien urged. "Ignore assholes throwing stones. We must focus on what we need to do."

"Right now, you need your strength. Once we help the spirits find closure, all of this," Lorna motioned toward the window, "will right itself."

"This should hold until I can have Sue fix it." Heather carried a board and plastic into the apartment. Jacob went to assist her.

"The shards are in the trash can when she does," Lorna said.

"It might be my menopause acting up, but the cold breeze feels nice." Vivien lifted her arms and stood in front of the window.

"I know where you are, bitch," a man yelled, his tone much gruffer than the first attacker.

Vivien dropped her arms. "Rude."

"You'll pay for what you've done," another man added.

Nina went toward the window and looked down at the street. She felt the others gathering behind her to watch.

"Careful," Jacob warned, placing his hand on her shoulder.

A man turned and walked away just as another strode into the middle of the street and stopped to look up at them.

"I see you!" The man pointed at them before finishing his way across to go down the sidewalk.

A car stopped in the street and the driver opened his door and lifted himself to glare at them from over the top of his sedan. He started to point but a cop car came up and flashed its lights. A small *blip-blip* of his siren sounded in warning. The man got back in his car and drove on.

The officer came forward to where the last man had been and got out of his cruiser. He looked up at Nina. "You'll be sorry. I'll make you pay!"

Nina leaned back. The officer got in his car and continued down the street as if nothing had happened.

"That's not a good sign," Vivien muttered.

"I'm going to venture a guess and say it's best if you don't go outside," Lorna added.

"I second that," Jacob agreed.

Nina watched the cop car's taillights to make sure he kept driving.

"Heather?" Vivien prompted. "Anything?"

Heather shook her head. "I don't see anyone. I mean, no one new. The guy sweeping the sidewalk and waving at nothing has been there forever."

Nina didn't see a guy sweeping the sidewalk.

"He died in the 1800s if the mustache is any indication," Heather explained. "He's a harmless residual. Not a bother to anyone."

"And maybe stay away from windows." Jacob took Nina by the shoulders and steered her back toward the food.

"Try this one." Lorna handed Nina a piece of a quesadilla.

"Come down here, you cowardly bitch. I dare you!" Yet another man yelled from outside.

Lorna motioned for Nina to eat. "Ignore it."

CHAPTER SIXTEEN

"H*I, Nina. This is Chance from Dr. Waters' office. She wanted me to call and tell you to go ahead and kill yourself. Have a good day.*"

Nina lowered the phone from her ear. Nothing should really surprise her by now, but she couldn't help the pang of fear returning to her chest. The possessions seemed to be popping up everywhere. How long until they took control of one of her new friends? Or Jacob, since all the possessed seemed to be males?

"What is it?" Vivien appeared in the doorway of Lorna's office where Nina checked her messages. Lorna had found her phone in the theater and charged it for her. "I felt a ripple. What happened?"

"Message from my doctor's office. I think they're canceling all my future appointments," Nina said.

"Don't worry. We'll find you a new doctor," Vivien motioned for Nina to come with her. "You ready?"

Nina deleted the message. "Yep."

She'd taken a shower and changed her clothes. It had helped her to feel human again. When contemplating her powers, she had managed to freeze the water streaming over her body. They'd felt like tiny shards, and thankfully the time stop hadn't lasted long.

Vivien took a bite of a burrito as they walked toward the theater. Seeing Nina watching, she winked. "Want a bite?"

"How can you still be eating? I don't understand where you put it all." Nina held up her hands. "Not that I'm trying to food shame you. It's just more of a modern mystery."

"It's awesome, isn't it?" Vivien grinned. "I mean, dealing with vengeful ghosts and psychic migraines all sucks ass, but at least there is one perk to being magical. All you can eat buffets are no longer a thing of the past. With all the good we try to put out into this world, I have to say karmically the universe owes us that much."

Vivien stopped and held up her hand for Nina to do the same before they entered the lobby.

"What?"

Vivien gestured around the corner. "Some of your fan club has been stopping by to glare into the front doors. We'll go straight to the theater. Just keep your head down."

Nina nodded.

Vivien led the way across the lobby. Nina couldn't help glancing toward the doors.

A large man who appeared as if he lived inside a gym instantly recognized her and began yelling obscenities. He started pounding on the door. The glass reverberated under his fists.

"Stop!" Nina yelled, covering her ears. "Just stop!"

The noise stopped.

She dropped her hands to see the man frozen mid-strike. His black gym shorts and tank top were rippled as if carved to indicate movement. The side of his fist pressed so hard into the glass that the skin had turned a shade of stark white.

"That is so cool." Vivien changed course for the door.

"Hey, Jacob's a statue," Heather said, coming out.

"What's going on out here? Why is Nina using her powers?"

Heather saw Vivien at the door and went to join her.

"Who invited Hercules to the party?" Heather asked.

"Clocks stopped," Lorna said, coming from behind the curtain with Sue.

"So did traffic." Heather tapped her finger on the glass to point outside.

"I would have killed for this power during algebra tests," Sue said.

Nina saw a white cat walk behind the angry statue. "Not the cat, though."

"That's Ace. He's special." Sue went to the door and opened it to let the cat come inside. "He runs the neighborhood."

"Meh," Ace meowed, sauntering past. He walked toward the back office as if he knew where he was going.

Nina watched the cat.

"He knows where we keep the snacks," Sue said.

"This guy is full of rage." Heather examined the bodybuilder through the door.

"Steroids," Vivien said. "He should knock that off. It'll shrink his balls, and then what is the point?"

"Let's get into the auditorium before you unfreeze him," Lorna suggested. "Out of sight will hopefully mean us out of his mind."

"Maybe we should go down to the coffee shop before you unfreeze him," Sue said.

Nina backed away from the door. "No. I won't leave Jacob."

"Of course not," Sue quickly amended. "You're right."

Nina led the way toward the amphitheater. Jacob was mid-action, hopping onto the front of the stage.

"You got to admit, he looks pretty cool like that," Vivien said.

"Yeah, Jacob always freezes in unique positions," Lorna teased. As she passed Nina, she gave her a slight nudge.

Nina cut through the chairs to the other side and made her way toward the stage. She stood near Jacob and willed him to move.

The bodybuilder's fists reverberated against the glass, accompanied by muffled shouts.

Jacob finished propelling himself onto the stage. Seeing Nina, he stumbled a little. "Where did you come from?"

The bodybuilder noise stopped.

"Magic," Vivien answered for her. She went to

peek past the curtains. "All clear. He's wandering off."

"Who?" Jacob asked.

"Would-be customer," Vivien dismissed. "Nothing to worry about."

"I'm confused." Jacob looked at all of them in turn. "What am I missing?"

"I should have mentioned the magic thing earlier," Nina answered, thinking of his stiff body on top of hers. She felt heat rising to her cheeks.

"You know how I can heal," Lorna joined them on the stage. "Heather sees ghosts. Sue does this..."

"Oh, uh," Sue looked around and lifted her hands. Pieces of spilled popcorn, candy wrappers, and soda cups lifted from beneath some of the seats. They floated in the air before making their way into a trash can.

"Sue cleans," Lorna said. "Kari teleports."

"Viv butts into people's business," Heather added.

"And I," Nina wasn't sure what to call her new gift, "make statues."

"Statues?" Jacob looked around the seating area.

"Stop," Nina ordered, lifting her hands.

"Stop what?" Jacob asked.

"Oh." Nina looked at her hands. "I thought that would work."

"It's intent, not a magic word," Vivien stated.

Nina concentrated on making the world stand still. Jacob stared at her, unmoving. She waited for a moment and then couldn't stop herself from touching his face. The subtle new growth of a beard didn't bend under her fingers.

"Everyone on the stage," Vivien said.

Nina stepped to the side, and they all gathered around her.

"Undo it," Heather said.

Nina willed the world to start again.

"The—" Jacob turned in surprise when Nina wasn't in front of him. "Where...?"

"Hi." Nina gave a small wave as he found them.

"Did you teleport?" he asked.

"I stopped time, and people, and cars," Nina tried to explain. "When I need time to take a breath, and I want them to stop, they do."

"Except us," Vivien said.

"That's..." Jacob didn't finish the thought.

"Super cool," Sue finished for him.

Jacob nodded, though that didn't appear to be what he'd meant to say.

Lorna went to a bag next to the séance cloth. She

pulled out cartons of blueberries and passed them around before opening one of her own.

"Didn't have time to put them into a muffin?" Vivien chuckled.

"No, we're going load up on all the protection we can get. Eat," Lorna ordered. She scooped a handful of blueberries into her mouth.

Everyone obeyed, not appearing to enjoy the snack as they hurried to swallow the berries.

Lorna held open the bag for them to discard their empty cartons.

Nina's phone began to ring in her pocket. She pulled it out and frowned to see Dr. Waters on the caller ID. She ignored the call and silenced the ringer.

"Nina?" Jacob held out his hand to her.

"It's no one," she said, sliding the phone back into her pocket.

Her phone began vibrating.

Jacob's hand hovered in the air between them. Nina took the offer, letting him pull her closer to him.

"Julia?" Heather called. "Grandma? Can you hear me?"

They waited in silence, listening to the theater.

"I can't find her," Heather said.

"It's only been three days," Lorna tried to sound comforting.

"Let's see if we can call her back." Vivien went to take her place around the cloth. "Maybe she needs a little boost."

Nina's phone again vibrated in her pocket. She tried to ignore it, but the idea that some stranger named Chance was calling to say hateful things filled her with anxiety.

"One second." Nina took her hand from Jacob's and pulled out her phone. She shut it down and then placed it on the stage floor away from the séancing area.

Jacob waited for her, and they walked to their places together. They joined hands. Energy flowed, connecting them.

"I haven't known you all long, but I feel closer to you than anyone," Nina said to the group. Their hair lifted over their head. "I'm sorry I brought this to your door."

"Nope," Heather shook her head. "You didn't bring anything to our door."

"None of this is your fault," Vivien added.

Nina nodded that she understood. She felt their sincerity. "Thank you for being my friends."

"Always," Heather said. "There's no getting rid of us now."

Nina turned to Jacob. "Thank you for always being here for me."

"You have to know," Jacob said. Warmth spread over her at his look. "You have to feel it."

"*Aww—*" Lorna started to react to the sweetness before catching herself.

"You have to see it," Jacob insisted. "I know I'm not good at hiding how I feel around you."

Nina felt his love rushing into her.

"Well, kiss him," Vivien insisted. "Say something."

Nina didn't break the circle. She gazed at him, willing him to feel what was inside her.

"To be continued." Jacob cleared his throat. "Shall we then, ladies?"

"Fine," Vivien grumbled.

"We intend to talk to Julia Warrick," Heather stated. The candle wicks erupted into flames. Nina gazed into Jacob's eyes while the others called forth the spirit to join them. When they stopped chanting, she finally looked into the circle. The overhead lights flickered.

"—in here?" Julia demanded loudly, appearing

between Heather and Vivien. Their hands were joined through her transparent body.

"In here?" Vivien asked.

"Who the blazes let you...?" Julia frowned and looked around. She still wore her 1920s outfit. "What happened? Why are you wearing different clothing?"

"You disappeared on us. It's been three days." Heather broke the circle and dropped her hands to her sides. "What happened?"

"What happened?" Julia repeated in disbelief. "You all decided to have a ghost party. This place was packed to the gills. They sucked the life out of the place. The entire block had a mini blackout. I didn't think I'd have to tell you not to invite the entire spiritual plain into one building. Especially not when they're sucking energy like it's a famine."

"We didn't realize there were so many," Nina said.

Julia turned her attention toward Nina. "Oh, there you are, storm cloud. You're looking much better. Little smokey but I can see your face now. You're not unsightly at all."

"Um, thanks. Nice to meet you, Ms. Warrick," Nina said, not sure what else to say. She let go of Lorna and Jacob and held out her hand to shake.

"Ick, no. Call me Julia." Julia ignored the offered hand and turned her attention toward Jacob. "I suppose we have you to thank for clearing those skies?"

"Excuse me?" Jacob glanced at Nina.

Julia laughed knowingly.

"Julia, behave," Heather warned.

"Why? She's right," Vivien inserted.

"I mean, I'm only assuming he's the reason she's all glowy. I guess it could have been that lurker," Julia quipped, gesturing off the stage.

They all turned in unison to stare at the empty seats.

"Heather?" Vivien asked.

"Nothing," Heather said.

"Julia, is someone else here with us?" Lorna asked.

"Um, not anymore." Julia moved toward the edge of the stage to look at the seats. She turned and gave a small jolt of surprise, startled. "Oh, wait. There he is."

Nina felt the hairs on the back of her neck stand up as Julia stared past her.

"Hiding behind the cloud," Julia said.

"I didn't know Teeter had male victims," Lorna said.

"I didn't either." Jacob reached for Nina's hand and slowly pulled her toward him. He wrapped his arms around her to keep her safe.

Nina shook as she looked to where she'd been standing. She didn't see anything.

"What does he look like?" Jacob asked.

"Trim beard," Julia said. "Leery. Like the unsettling guy who sits in the corner of the speakeasy and stares at all the ladies without talking to them. The one you don't want to follow you to the parking lot."

"It can't be." Nina pushed away from Jacob and hurried for her phone. She kept looking around, trying to sense where the figure hid.

Jacob rushed after her. Nina turned on her phone.

"What are you doing?" he asked.

"Looking..." She tapped her fingers impatiently, alternating between glancing at the screen as it loaded and keeping an eye out for the invisible man.

She had the strongest urge to run. The echo of the past filled her with the *thump, thump, thump* of her bare feet on wet pavement until she realized it was the sound of her finger tapping the side of the cell phone. A notification for six missed calls appeared. She ignored them all.

The screen lit, and she instantly pulled up the internet to type in a search, *"Robert Teeter death."*

Articles about his victims popped up, the newest speculating about the bodies being recovered near a yellow barn and how authorities weren't commenting.

"It's not him," Nina whispered in relief. She looked at the others and showed them her phone screen. "It's not Teeter. There is nothing about him dying in the news. He's not a ghost."

"Julia, have you seen the bearded man before?"

"Yes, at the last séance," Julia said.

"Teeter was still locked up when I talked to my friend earlier," Jacob confirmed. "He is alive."

"So, it can't be him," Nina stated again, waiting for everyone to agree with her. "He's behind bars."

"Not dead, huh." Julia hooked her thumbs into her front pockets and nodded. "That explains it."

"Explains what?" Heather asked. "You're going to have to be a little more forthcoming here, Grandma."

Julia frowned at the name. "Do I look like a grandma?"

"*Julia*, explain," Heather insisted.

"He's more of a dead spot. Spirits take energy from their surroundings, even when they're not manifesting. This one is..." Julia tilted her head and frowned. "He's like a movie projection. The energy is emanating from the source, not being sucked into the image."

"We dealt with that before," Sue said. "Spirits using movies to get across their messages."

"Only, he's not prerecorded." Julia crossed her arms over her chest. "There's darkness there."

"Do you mean demonic?" Lorna visibly shivered.

Julia glared at a spot near Nina. "Hey! Yeah, you, lurker boy. What are you doing here?"

Nina whimpered and instantly moved closer to Jacob. Lorna and Sue came to stand beside them. The three of them created a shield around her. Heather and Vivien went toward Julia.

Nina held up her phone toward Julia to show a picture of Teeter. "Is this him?"

Julia's image flickered, and she appeared before Nina. She had aged within seconds. Her makeup faded into a subtler shade. Her hair shortened and curled around her head. Her trousers and shirt morphed into a floral dress.

"Girls, get out," Julia ordered, not giving Nina an answer. "Get out of here now."

"What?" Vivien frowned.

Julia gasped and looked around the theater.

A loud crash sounded in the lobby. The sound of shattered glass tinkled unmistakably. Julia disappeared only to reappear in the aisle below.

A loud growl rang out.

"Hide." Jacob nudged Nina toward Lorna before leaping off the stage. He ran along the aisle toward the front.

"No!" Nina yelled.

She jumped off the side of the stage. When she landed, a burning sensation overtook her foot and ankle. It was enough to delay her a few seconds. Jacob was through the curtains by the time she resumed her chase. She limped for a few steps before she was able to return to a normal gait.

A loud crash sounded, followed by a man's scream.

"Nina!" Vivien called as if trying to stop her. "Be careful!"

Nina wouldn't leave Jacob to fight alone. She pushed through the curtains.

The bodybuilder who'd been banging on the door had breached the lobby. He stood next to the broken concessions and held the popcorn machine over his head. He hefted it at Jacob.

"Watch out!" Nina yelled.

Jacob dove out of the way.

The bodybuilder turned his attention to her.

"Get out of here," Julia ordered.

At first, Nina thought the ghost was yelling at her. The bodybuilder pivoted toward 1920s Julia, evidently able to see and hear the spirit. He lifted his arms and roared at her.

Julia charged the man, screeching like a banshee as she dove into his body. She appeared out of the other side, gripping a shadowy figure.

The bodybuilder dropped his arms and stumbled. He looked around in confusion before darting out of the broken door.

Nina's shoes crunched on the broken glass covering the floor as she went to Jacob. She helped him to his feet. Julia struggled with the shadow, their images flickering and reappearing in different locations around the lobby.

"Nina," Lorna yelled, waving her toward the curtain and away from the fight.

"Sue, you got this?" Vivien appeared on the other side of the concessions.

"On it." Sue flung her arms. The glass shards on the floor flew toward the broken door, rebuilding themselves into the window like a puzzle.

Jacob moaned softly in surprise as tiny shards

were pulled out of his forearm to help fix the door. He examined the cuts that remained behind.

Sue then waved her hand toward the broken display case. It righted itself but was much slower at doing so. She took a deep breath and leaned against the case as if she'd overexerted herself.

Nina led Jacob around the dented popcorn machine toward the curtains.

"Where's Julia?" Heather asked.

"I don't see her," Vivien said.

"Did you see that thing she was fighting?" Heather went down the corridor toward Lorna's office before coming back. "She's not down there."

"Did anyone see me fix the window?" Sue asked, not leaving the display case. "I forgot to check outside first."

"I don't think so," Nina answered, though she didn't know for sure. "The street looked empty."

Lorna went behind the counter and pulled out a candy bar. She slid it toward Sue.

Nina lifted Jacob's arm to look at it in the light. "We need bandages."

"I'll be all right," Jacob dismissed the concern.

"Get back to the book," Heather said. "There is a bad energy in here. We need to make sure we don't leave any doorways open between our world and wherever that monster is coming through."

"But what if we didn't open a door? What if there is no metaphorical door? How do we close something that isn't even there?" Vivien waited for everyone to follow Heather through the curtains before taking up the rear. "He was coming before Nina found that ring. If he's not a ghost...?"

"How do we stop a man already in prison? Can we even get access to where he's being held?" Lorna asked. "And if we do, what then? Sending ghosts and demons on their way isn't the same as offing some guy in his cell."

"Easy, Folsom Prison," Vivien said. "We're not shanking anyone in their cell."

"If Vivien says no, it must be a bad idea," Sue said.

"Well...?" Lorna gestured helplessly.

"At least not yet," Vivien amended.

"He's projecting himself," Heather said. "I think it's some kind of psychic teleport or possession or mind control. Jacob, what do you know about where they're holding him?"

"He's under heavy supervision. I've been told if he's not meditating in his cell, he's been rambling about weird shit and freaking the other prisoners out," Jacob said.

"Like what?" Heather asked.

"He climbed on top of a table in the dining hall and claimed he could defy gravity. He demanded a bunch of bikers bow down to him, or he'd give them nightmares," Jacob said. "Nonsense like that. They figured he's angling for an insanity plea."

"Meditating? Astral projection?" Nina asked. "Is that real?"

"Kind of like that," Heather said. "But I think astral travel means they're in the astral plane where spirits reside, but this guy is affecting our reality. He's possessing people and making them torment you. That's something else. He's sending his spirit out into the world, but I don't know how he's doing it. Without a soul, the body dies."

"What if he doesn't have a soul?" Nina had looked into his eyes. All that had been there was a sick glee in the pain of others. There was no compassion within that nightmare of a man.

"It might not be much of one, but he has a soul," Vivien said. "He's just a man. Men can be beaten."

"Julia!" Heather yelled, returning to the stage where the cloth and book were laid out. "We need you. Now!"

CHAPTER SEVENTEEN

"The candles are almost burned out," Lorna observed as they sat in the row of seats in front of the stage. They had been waiting on the floor around the cloth, but the wooden slats proved to be too hard for comfort. Nina generally didn't think of herself as old and falling apart but sitting on hard surfaces seemed like a form of torture on her mature hips and lower back.

No one seemed to know what to do, so they waited in hopes that Julia might return. Nina leaned her head against Jacob's shoulder, finding comfort in his nearness. Vivien and Heather whispered for a long time amongst themselves but didn't feel the need to share the conversation with the others.

Heather flipped through the pages in search of

answers. Frowning, she slammed it shut. "I can't find anything in here."

"Everything I'm finding online isn't useful to our situation," Vivien added, flicking her finger against her phone screen. She wore a pair of reading glasses as she surfed the internet for clues.

"What?" Heather drawled wryly. "There isn't a video tutorial on how to kill a locked up serial killer who is tormenting your friend with his mind while meditating in prison?"

"Surprisingly, no." Vivien clicked off her phone and pulled the glasses from her face. "But there are about fifty billion ways to use meditation to reduce stress. None of them included binging on chocolate cake, so I'm pretty sure they're all bogus."

Nina wasn't sure how she felt about watching them search for answers. She had hoped they would just know what to do. Like when you went to a dentist to have an extraction. In, out, and over. Though she could hardly resent the fact they were trying to help. It's not like she had answers to give.

"I just want this to be over," Nina whispered. Jacob tightened his hold on her.

"I have more candles in the office," Lorna said. "I should get those. Looks like we're going to need them."

"I'll go with you." Sue stood. "I need the restroom."

"Don't go anywhere alone," Vivien ordered.

"And don't be gone long," Heather added, before yelling after them as they went past the curtains, "Watch the front doors!"

Nina lifted her head from Jacob's shoulder. "I'm so sorry about this—"

"Nope," Heather interrupted.

"Stop," Vivien said at the same time. "Not your fault."

"I'm calling Martin." Heather handed the book to Vivien. "I want to tell them we'll be later than planned. I don't want them showing up here worried. He's been stressed out enough lately without me piling on."

"They'll all be worried." Vivien placed the book on her lap. "They always worry. They try to hide it, so I let them think I don't know, but our hobby is hard on them."

"Still, I don't want them coming near this place. That bastard seems to like possessing males. Let's not give him any." Heather looked at Jacob. "That includes you. If you start to feel funny, you say something."

Jacob nodded.

"Do you feel all right?" Nina asked him.

"I don't think anyone is trying to take over my mind if that's what you're asking," he said. "Although I don't like this waiting."

"We have to give Julia a chance to come back." Vivien opened the book and put her glasses back on.

Nina heard Heather on the phone with her boyfriend. The woman wandered through the seats as she talked, lightly shaking them as if looking for loose bolts.

Nina put her hand on Jacob's chest and gazed up at him. "I feel like I want to say thank you again."

"You don't have to." He grinned, glancing at her mouth. "I'd rather you thank me later. Properly."

"I can do that." Nina leaned toward him, letting her lips brush against his.

Before they could deepen the kiss, Vivien mumbled teasingly, "Get a room."

"We had a room," Jacob said, his voice lowering an octave.

Nina started to laugh in surprise, but when she looked into his eyes, she realized something was wrong.

He gripped her arm, squeezing tight. "Don't you remember? I know you do. I'm in your dreams. You keep me there with you."

Nina shot up from her chair and tore her arm from his grasp.

"Jacob?" Nina studied his face, lifting a hand between them to push at his chest. She jerked her arm from his grasp. "Jacob, look at me. Are you—?"

"I have to go. Call you later." Heather hung up the phone.

"In here now!" Vivien yelled.

Heather hurried through a row of chairs before running down the aisle. Sue and Lorna appeared from behind the curtain.

"He's possessed Jacob," Vivien said. "Nina back toward me. Quickly."

Nina didn't want to leave Jacob's side, but she didn't know what else to do.

"Teeter?" Nina could barely get the name out of her mouth.

"I prefer *Dr.* Teeter, thank you," Jacob's possessed voice answered.

"I prefer asshole," Vivien muttered. She grabbed Nina's arm and forcibly shoved her up the stairs onto the stage.

"Leave him alone," Nina ordered.

Teeter laughed. The sound gave her chills. Jacob's voice no longer sounded like his. "Did you really think you could hide from me, lucky number seven? Don't you understand yet? We're linked. You belong to me. You and all my angels I plucked from heaven. I chose you and you belong to me."

"No, I don't believe that." Nina shook her head. She remembered Teeter being a talker, always going on about numbers and destiny. The words were carried in the fog of her memory.

"Keep him talking," Heather whispered. "Distract him."

Lorna placed candles on the floor next to the piles of blue wax that had almost burned completely out. Vivien set the book in the middle of the séancing cloth.

Nina struggled with what to say. "How did you find me? How are you here?"

Teeter took a step forward, the movement jerky, as if trying to find the right controls to his new vehicle. "You've heard of the seventh son, haven't you?"

Nina shook her head.

"The seventh son of the seventh son," Teeter stated in loud annoyance as if raising his voice would help her magically understand his nonsense.

"Sure," Heather said. "I read about that. The seventh son of the seventh son, with no girls born in between, is supposed to produce some kind of rare psychic. It's folklore."

"It's real!" Teeter announced. "All my life people have dismissed me, told me my powers were in my imagination. But I had the mark. Seven birthmarks. I am the seventh son of the seventh son *of the seventh son*. I was born from three generations of greatness and destined to be an extraordinary doctor like those seventh sons before me. I had the propensity, but then my father died, and with seven children and a squandered fortune, my mother couldn't afford to send me to medical school."

"Doctors heal people," Nina reasoned. "You hurt them."

"Doctors are god," Teeter corrected. "No one questions them. Give him this pill. Lock him in a room. Attach electrodes to his head and shock the delusions out of him."

His steps became steadier, and he began moving with increased speed.

"Bow down to your god, my seventh angel," he ordered Nina. "It's time to take your place in my pantheon."

"Fuck you," Nina yelled.

"We intend to call Julia Warrick," Heather stated.

Teeter scoffed.

"Get out of him," Nina said. "Jacob has nothing to do with us."

Teeter made it to the stairs and started the climb toward her. "Don't worry. I'll walk him off the top of this building just as soon as I'm done here. After I finish with you, I think I see my next four playthings ready for my attention. Prison will not stop me from my destiny."

"Come and get it, you sick fuck," Heather taunted.

Vivien grabbed Nina's hand and pulled her into a circle with the others. The candle flames burned low, their light dimming.

"Don't hurt Jacob," Nina begged the women as she took Lorna's hand.

"I told you to get out!" Julia appeared from the shadows in the back of the theater, flying over the seats as she dove at Teeter. The overhead lights turned off with a loud popping noise.

The faint image of Julia disappeared inside Jacob's body, only to reemerge with Teeter's dark shadow. The low candles blew out. The spirits passed by Nina's body, causing her to gasp as the cold blast sent an ache through her entire frame. Julia and Teeter landed inside the circle of symbols. The new candles flamed higher than should have been possible from their wicks.

"Julia, get out!" Heather commanded.

Nina felt a pull at her energy as if someone stood behind her. She turned her head to the side to find Nancy wearing her hospital gown outside of the circle. The ghost touched Nina's shoulder.

Julia somersaulted, rolling between Vivien and Heather. Teeter tried to follow her. He hit the barrier of the cloth symbols like an invisible wall and was shoved back. He charged the barrier several times, bouncing off it with outraged cries.

Another ghost appeared next to Nancy and placed a hand on Nancy's shoulder, and then another appeared beside that one. Each spirit joined in the circle, their transparent forms spiraling around Nina and her friends.

"Being tethered in our net," Julia stated as she pushed up from the ground. She stood with her arms wide as the victim's ghost included her in their spiral. "Time for you to take what you get. We send you to your eternal hell. Pay the price with this final knell."

The ghosts began to scream, releasing all the pain and rage that kept them trapped to the earth. Nina felt it ringing inside her, and she joined them, crying out from the deepest depths of her soul.

Teeter held his hands over his ears. His mouth opened, but the others drowned out the sound of his screams. The flames surged, joining like a net over him before crashing down on his head. Black ash collapsed onto the cloth, scorching the material.

Instantly, the screaming stopped. Nina felt like a dark weight had been lifted from inside her. She turned to look at Nancy. The hospital gown was gone. The woman wore a sundress, and her translucent face appeared golden as if the sun shone through her.

Nancy tilted her head once and smiled. Nina reached for the hand on her shoulder, but Nancy burst into tiny lights. The others followed suit, lighting up the stage like dancing stars.

"They're beautiful," Lorna whispered.

"Go in peace and love," Heather said.

Nina felt tears rolling down her cheeks. She fell to her knees and stared up at the leaving women. She felt their freedom, their lightness. When the last light faded, all that was left were the candles. They flickered like normal around the scorched cloth. The smell of burned material scented the air.

"Jacob." Nina crawled to where he had fallen on the stage. She leaned over him and touched his warm face. "Wake up. Come on, baby, wake up. Look at me."

He moaned softly.

Nina leaned over to kiss the corner of his mouth. "Open your eyes."

"What the hell was that?" He grunted, grabbing his head.

"You ladies keep a gal on her toes. That's enough excitement for—" Julia's voice suddenly stopped, and the lights came back on, though not as bright as before.

"We need new bulbs," Lorna said. "Three are blown out."

"We need a new séancing blanket," Vivien added.

"I think I need a new shoulder," Sue said, rubbing her arm. "I ran into the bathroom door, trying to rush in here. But, fuck, that was amazing. I feel like I'm high."

Heather gave a small chuckle and caught herself until Vivien started in. They both began laughing, prompting Sue and Lorna to join them. A giddy sense of accomplishment filled the air.

"Take that, you asshole!" Sue yelled down at the burned cloth.

The women laughed harder.

Nina grinned at Jacob, pulling on his arm to help him sit. "We did it. He's gone. Can't you feel it?"

Jacob looked around in slight confusion. "Did I miss it?"

"I would say you played an important role." Heather stood over him. "Sorry I couldn't tell you the plan earlier. If you knew it was coming, you wouldn't have been susceptible to trapping Teeter where we could find him."

"You used him as bait," Nina frowned, about to apologize to him.

"I knew he wouldn't mind," Vivien said. "Julia needed him to get Teeter near the circle. We had to trap him where we could find him. This was the only way we could think of."

"She's right. I would have said yes to anything to save you," he said. "I love you, Nina. I know you know that."

Love? Nina felt absolutely no fear in that word or in the future.

"I love you, too," Nina cupped his face in her hands and kissed him. Words would never seem enough to express all she wanted to say to him.

"Hey, didn't we have chocolate cake upstairs?" Vivien asked.

Heather grabbed the book. Sue grabbed the

edges of the singed cloth and rolled it into a ball around the ashes. "I'm going to go put this somewhere safe."

"Where's that? A dumpster?" Vivien asked.

"Cemetery seems about right," Sue said. "Not sure if the hallowed ground will matter, but it sounds good."

"I'll drive with you," Heather moved to follow her. Before they left, she yelled, "Save me some cake."

Jacob held her hand as they walked toward the upstairs apartment.

"Is anyone else hungry?" Lorna asked. "Should we order a pizza?"

"Dibs on the leftover tacos." Vivien took the stairs to the apartment two at a time.

"Hey." Jacob stopped Nina from following them up.

Nina wrapped her arms around his neck and smiled. "Hey."

Jacob planted a kiss on her mouth before stroking a lock of her hair away from her cheek. "I need to ask you something important."

"Anything." Nina placed her hand over his heart, feeling it beat under her palm.

"Do you think they'll still respect me if I ask for a

salad?" he whispered. "Because I can't keep eating like I'm fourteen. Their diet is going to do me in."

Nina laughed. "I honestly don't know how they do it. We'll both ask for a salad. Maybe they won't notice."

Jacob grinned, pulling her against him. "I need to kiss you now."

Nina wrapped her arms around his neck and offered her lips. The memories of what she had been through were there inside of her, but they no longer affected her. She was completely free.

CHAPTER EIGHTEEN

EPILOGUE

"SERIAL KILLER ROBERT CHESTER TEETER, *who had been pronounced brain dead last week, was taken off life support. Teeter was found unresponsive last Tuesday morning inside his prison cell. Authorities are unsure what caused the coma but have assured the public in an earlier press conference that investigations are underway to protect the health and safety of all prisoners."*

Jacob closed the news site and placed his tablet on the coffee table. "It's over."

Nina leaned her head against his shoulder as she curled next to him on the couch. "Thank goodness that is one dark spirit we don't have to worry about manifesting ever again."

Heather had offered the Warrick Theater apartment to them for as long as they wanted, without cost. She could tell her new friends wanted her to stay permanently in Freewild Cove, but she needed to move back to Sallyville. She had unfinished living to do.

"The world is a better place," Jacob said. "The DA has asked me to have you come in to review a few details so they can close the file. They're notifying the families. He promised to pass them the message from Cady to her husband. I said it came up in our conversations about what happened."

Nina felt an immense sadness at the thought of the others, but also a comfort. Whenever the evil thoughts tried to invade, she remembered the look of them leaving and finding peace. She felt them inside her and would forever carry them with her.

"The office has also been fielding book and documentary offers," he said. "They're willing to pay big for the story."

"No." Nina shook her head. She looked at where their packed bags were piled near the stairwell. "I have a good job. I drive a bus for the school district. Besides, who'd believe any of the crazy stuff that happened here?"

"I was asked to pass the offer along," he said,

rubbing his hand up and down her arm. "Are you sure you want to go back there?"

"I like Freewild Cove and love my new friends, but my home is in Sallyville. I want to get back to it." She smiled and held up her hand to look at the oval ring on her middle finger. "Besides, it's only a forty-minute drive. If they need me, I'll feel it, and I'll come back."

"*Our* home is in Sallyville," he corrected. "Don't think I forgot about your moving in with me."

"Did we decide that?" she teased, trying not to laugh. "Maybe I'm still considering options."

"Joke all you want, but I have the keys to the moving truck. I've been needing to buy new dishware, so those boxes are coming with me regardless."

"Well, when you make it sound so romantic..." Nina kissed him. "How can I refuse?"

Jacob leaned toward her, forcing her onto her back on the couch. "You think that's romantic, what until I tell you about the flat screen television and unlimited sports package you'll be gaining."

"Be still my heart." Nina laughed.

"Never still," he countered. "I want to make it race."

Joy bubbled up inside of her. She had learned what it meant to be truly happy, and to let go of her demons. Life might not offer perfection, but it offered hope. And she had great hope in the future.

"Come here, you." Nina pulled him into her embrace and intended never to let go.

The End

GET THE BOOKS!

The Magical Fun Continues!

Lorna's Story:
Order of Magic Book 1: Second Chance Magic

Vivien's Story:
Order of Magic Book 2: Third Time's a Charm

Heather's Story:
Order of Magic Book 3: The Fourth Power

Sue's Story:
Order of Magic Book 4: The Fifth Sense

Kari's Story:
Order of Magic Book 5: The Sixth Spell

Nina's Book:
Order of Magic Book 6: The Seventh Key

The Next Book
Order of Magic Book 7: The Eighth Potion

ABOUT MICHELLE M. PILLOW

New York Times **& USA TODAY**
Bestselling Author

Michelle loves to travel and try new things, whether it's a paranormal investigation of an old Vaudeville Theatre or climbing Mayan temples in Belize. She believes life is an adventure fueled by copious amounts of coffee.

Newly relocated to the American South, Michelle is involved in various film and documentary projects with her talented director husband. She is mom to a fantastic artist. And she's managed by a dog and cat who make sure she's meeting her deadlines.

For the most part she can be found wearing pajama pants and working in her office. There may or may not be dancing. It's all part of the creative process.

Come say hello! Michelle loves talking with readers on social media!

www.MichellePillow.com

- facebook.com/AuthorMichellePillow
- twitter.com/michellepillow
- instagram.com/michellempillow
- bookbub.com/authors/michelle-m-pillow
- goodreads.com/Michelle_Pillow
- amazon.com/author/michellepillow
- youtube.com/michellepillow
- pinterest.com/michellepillow

NEWSLETTER

To stay informed about when a new book in the
series installments is released, sign up for updates:

Sign up for Michelle's Newsletter

michellepillow.com/author-updates

PLEASE LEAVE A REVIEW

THANK YOU FOR READING!

Please take a moment to share your thoughts by reviewing this book.

Be sure to check out Michelle's other titles at www.MichellePillow.com

www.ingramcontent.com/pod-product-compliance
Lightning Source LLC
Chambersburg PA
CBHW020123120726
47903CB00007B/2078